KAIRN

MATES
OF THE
ALLIANCE

BOOK 1

FIONNE FOXXE FARRADAY

Jan-Carol
Publishing, Inc
"every story needs a book"

Kairn: Mates of the Alliance
Fionne Foxxe Farraday
Published September 2022
Broken Crow Ridge
Imprint of Jan-Carol Publishing, Inc.
All rights reserved
Copyright © 2022 Fionne Foxxe Farraday
Cover Design: Peter Ochabski

ISBN: 978-1-954978-63-8
E-ISBN: 978-1-954978-47-8
Library of Congress Control Number: 2022946277

Jan-Carol Publishing, Inc.
PO Box 701
Johnson City, TN 37605
publisher@jancarolpublishing.com
www.jancarolpublishing.com

For all the hopeful souls looking
for their very own Kairn, never settle.
Your person—your mate—is out there
and will be well worth the wait.

LETTER TO THE READER

Fighting to save a primitive planet targeted by the Alliance's enemies, Kairn never expected to find the female who haunted his dreams made flesh and blood.

Daria's life revolved around her work. She had given up on finding romance...let alone love. Earth was now under attack by an evil alien empire—under siege. Daria is trying to do her job as best she can in an upside-down world. Then the cavalry arrives...in the form of giant, gorgeous alien warriors.

These aliens are working toward restoring Earth to the pristine beauty she used to be. In their charismatic leader, Daria finds the most amazing partner. What's an Earth girl to do but grab on with both hands and hold on tight to enjoy the ride? After all...what could possibly go wrong?

Kairn: Mates of the Alliance is full of exciting battle scenes and sweet, steamy romance. This book is intended for mature audiences only. Italics within the story denote a character's thoughts or words spoken in another language, including languages that may not be human.

I hope you have as much fun reading about Daria and Kairn's adventures as I had writing about them. I would love to read your reviews on social media or online—anywhere the book can be purchased.

PROLOGUE

Daria at Age 16

Daria scribbled notes in the margins as the teacher highlighted the finer points of calculus. She nibbled absently on the end of her mechanical pencil. The bell rang, signifying the end of the class.

Taking her time, Daria gathered her textbook. She pushed her glasses back up. Her long hair fell into her face. Daria absently pulled her hair back in a high ponytail. The room was emptying quickly of the college freshmen. AP Calc was proving to be a lonely place for a precocious high school junior.

Slinging her backpack over her shoulder, she joined the students in the crowded corridor. She saw pretty college girls flirting with attentive frat boys. Daria mused to herself ruefully, *How can it be possible to feel so alone in a sea of people?*

Daria glanced down at her comfortable jeans, sneakers, and favorite AC/DC T-shirt. She twirled the ends of her ponytail as she looked at the straightened hair, subtle make-up, and body-slimming clothes of the sorority girls. One of the girls shifted her feet, cocking her hip with a flirty kick of her high-heeled foot. Her fresh French pedicure peeked out provocatively from the very pretty torture instruments she sported on her abused feet.

Daria shuddered. *I don't think I'm missing much there.*

As Daria watched, one of the boys leaned forward. He tucked a few errant curls behind the girl's ears with careful fingers. The girl stopped flirting, blushing prettily. The boy—young man, really—took the book bag the girl passed to him. Her cheeks heating to a soft rose, she flashed him a shy smile. Offering her his crooked elbow, the pair walked down the hall with their heads tilted close together...oblivious to the rest of the world.

Charmed by their obvious sweet chemistry, Daria glanced after the pair with a wistful smile. The bell rang again, shaking her out of her reverie. *I don't have time for this. Focus, girl. Finish high school...then college...then med school. Time to stop feeling sorry for myself.*

She walked down the hall, hurrying to her next AP class. *I do get a little lonely...okay, a lot. I wish I had someone...I want to be close to someone...one day. I hope there's someone out there just for me.*

Daria—present day

The soft-pitched drawl fell pleasantly on her ears.

"I think I'm ready to head home, Ma'am."

Daria pulled her stethoscope out of her ears. She smiled warmly at the distinguished older gentleman sitting ramrod straight in the bedside chair.

"You sound clear today, Mr. Clark. I do believe you're right. I'll get started on your discharge order. If you drive like you usually do, you should be home with your missus for supper."

A quick grin flashed across his weathered features. He stood politely and bowed slightly as Daria headed toward the door. "I surely appreciate all you did for me. Have a care going home on those roads. Pet your hoss of a dog for me."

Daria heard Mr. Clark dialing his cell phone before she even turned for the door. She heard him chuckle. "Sweetheart, they're cutting me loose outta this popsicle stand. I'll be home with you soon, darling girl."

Daria smiled whimsically to herself as she closed the door gently behind her.

She nodded to the charge nurse, Jenny. "Mr. Clark is headed out the door. You'd better hurry if you want to keep up with him."

Laughter rang out around the station. "We'd better get on it before he makes a break for it."

Dalton Clark was one of Daria's favorite people. She always made a point to finish her rounds with him before she left for the day. Barring any emergencies, he was always her last stop if he was in the hospital. Daria smiled to herself. *It was always good to end the day on a high note.*

Sneakers squeaking, Daria headed down the back stairs and walked to the parking lot. She tucked her wavy brown hair behind her ears. Daria saw Nils Larsen, a good friend and dedicated surgeon. He was talking with Laura, one of the hospital recruiters. He looked up as the stairwell door closed behind Daria. He grinned and lifted his chin at Daria.

Nils leaned closer to Laura with a smile. Her manicured fingers played with the gold necklace laying across the hollow of her throat. Laura wound a lock of black hair around her finger. They laughed softly. Daria heard him murmur, "Meet you there in an hour."

Nils put a guiding hand on the small of her back as he walked Laura to her car and helped her in. Nils stared after Laura for a few moments as she drove off.

Daria smiled at Nils as he got into his SUV. She could see the sparks of attraction between them. Daria made a shooing motion. "She's sweet. I like her. What are you waiting for?"

Nils laughed as he started his engine. As he reversed, he stuck his head out the window. "Hey, Morrissey. Good job today. Thanks for your help."

He paused, a faraway look in his eyes. His voice was soft. "I like her too."

Daria took her time on the winding roads home. She had the moonroof open with the cool sea-kissed air blowing through her hair. The stunning views along the mountain curves and the sound of the crashing surf blew the last of the cobwebs from her mind.

Daria took the nearly invisible turn-off into the winding gravel road leading up to her home. The familiar rumble of her engine brought inquisitive squirrels out to investigate. Chittering with excited curiosity, they ran along the crisscrossing branches forming a living archway along the trail.

Excited barks greeted her. The sound of dancing feet on the hardwood floor made her smile and relax even more. Opening the front door, Daria let Molly out for a good run.

With a grin, Daria followed, watching her dog run sprints across the meadow as the sun set. She wriggled her toes in the tall grass. With a happy sigh, she headed into her cozy home. She luxuriated in a lovely, long as-hot-as-she-could-stand-it bath in the deep, old-fashioned copper tub. Fragrant steam filled the bathroom with the relaxing scents of lavender and chocolate. She ate a simple dinner and fed the last of her Reuben sandwich to a hopeful Molly. *Who knew dogs would love sauerkraut?*

Daria sunk into the comfortably worn sofa, rubbing a lazy foot along Molly's side. The big shepherd mix wagged her tail lazily in expressive thanks. Leaning back into the soft cushions, Daria cuddled under the oversized throw. She stared absently into the peaceful room, the soft crackle and pop of the fire lulling her into a light doze.

Daria thought about Nils and Laura. She had a good feeling about them. A sharp pang of loneliness crept over her, foreign and contrary to her usual easygoing, happy nature. Her gaze drifted to the large empty spot at the other end of the sofa. Daria let out a wistful sigh. *What would it be like to have someone special to share this with?*

A soft woof broke the strange spell and drew her eyes to an alert Molly. Once Molly was sure she was the sole focus of her human's attention, she promptly lolled expectantly onto her back. Daria laughed, sinking down onto the smooth old oak floors to give Molly a world-class belly rub.

Daria was rewarded by a riotous symphony of happy high-pitched yips and whines. She watched with fond amusement as her huge shepherd reverted to puppyhood and crawled into her lap. Daria teased affectionately, "You spoiled little thing!"

And scratched some more.

Some hours later...

Daria startled awake out of a fitful sleep. Disoriented, she sat up on her makeshift bed, her pulse pounding loudly in her ears. Nails clicked on the wooden floor as Molly growled, hackles rising as she planted herself squarely in front of the door.

The dying embers in the fireplace cast eerie flickering shadows as Daria's eyes adjusted to the dark room. She listened intently, straining her ears. Nothing except Molly's continued deep growl broke the silence.

She stroked a gentle hand along Molly's silky ears. "Easy girl. What's got you all stirred up?"

The large dog shook herself and stared fixedly at the door, hackles standing up along her spine.

Daria didn't hear anything, but she trusted her dog implicitly. A shiver ran through her. That was it. They were in her beyond-rustic cabin in the mountains. Secluded and peaceful. But now the usual voices of the night were eerily silent. No owls. No yipping coyotes in the distance. No crickets. It had been a great place to recharge, but now it was TOO quiet.

With exaggerated care, Daria swung the heavy door open to avoid its habitual squeak, Molly posting protectively at her side. Easing through the doorway, Daria stared at the red glow highlighting the early dawn. Dull, menacing booming sounded, repeated, and echoed.

A brilliant light exploded along the horizon before subsiding into an angry red glare. As far as Daria could see, the skies were on fire. In the distance, cities were burning.

Multiple jet engines roared over her head. Daria thought wildly, *Please God, let those be our jets!*

The powerful unseen craft flew low and fast toward the cities.

CHAPTER ONE

Kairn

Kairn slowly opened his eyes. He struggled to recall the fading details of his dream. Every night had been like this for the last four hands. Vivid dreams...more like visions. They had started out as snapshots in her life. She had been young and adorably awkward in the first one...still in classes. Later dreams showed her hard at work. Relaxing at home. At play. Eyes bright with laughter. Every dream crackled with her bright energy. It was the same female each time. *His* female.

The last hand of nights were different. The tone was darker and violent. Of late, the view from her tidy little house had changed. It was the same landscape in the distance, but the hither-to-peaceful background was now being ravaged by flame. Alarms blared in the background.

Controlled voices shouted as order was established out of the swirling chaos—but he could hear the undercurrent of fear in their strained tones.

Kairn did not know if these visions were a sign of things that were in her past, present, or future. He was desperately hoping for future events he could prevent or ameliorate. He felt a headache throb to life as he pondered the possibilities.

Kairn propped himself against the wall, his tail flicking absently. He frowned as he stared unseeing at the spectacular stars glimmering peacefully against the background of space, lost in thought. His comm crackled to life, drawing him out of his reverie. "Commander to bridge."

Kairn arrived on the bridge, drawing the alert attention of his crew. The GUARDIAN was battle proven and the flagship for the battle group; his veteran crew had been with him for many rotations. They had all bonded through a slew of hard-won victories against the Ichori hordes.

His science officer and XO, Darzik, was an old friend. Darzik gave him a sharp knowing glance. Apparently, his lack of sleep was becoming evident on his already lean face. Darzik was succinct as always. "Urgent communique from Central Command. The Ichori have amassed an invasion fleet. We are being dispatched to intercept—and to ensure that the Ichori do not establish a base in this system."

Kairn nodded his acknowledgment as he scanned the holodata. The Alliance had designated this a closed world; her people had not yet achieved interstellar travel. This planet was fragmented by regional governments, each driven by their own petty, selfish objectives. It was fraught with endless wars spurred by religious and meaningless superficial differences in physical traits. The world was blessed with an abundance of natural resources, but its atmosphere and environment were tainted with willful byproducts of blind mass industry. The planet's land masses were blighted with large depositories of non-biodegradable matter...an eyesore even from the depths of space.

This was a world bitterly divided...in the face of a merciless amoral enemy. They did not stand a chance. Kairn frowned darkly. *What could they have that has captured the malignant unwavering interest of the Ichori?*

A vid of the planet shimmered into vivid, beguiling life. Kairn stared fixedly at the screen as dark understanding dawned: Her surface was a kaleidoscope of brilliant colors, but most of it was a deep hypnotizing blue.

Countless unsuspecting, hapless lives. Kairn snarled, "Plot a course for the battle group at attack speed and calculate coordinates for nearest wormhole exiting into or near that solar system."

He looked at the hologram of the primitive planet. *Gods help the poor bastards. Most of their planet was priceless Water.*

CHAPTER TWO

Molly was barking frantically. Daria hurried up the well-worn path and fumbled the door open, only to be knocked nearly flat as Molly launched herself at her. Daria laughed through happy tears as her 115-pound German Shepherd mix crawled into her lap. "Everything's okay, girl. Happy to see you too."

Daria nudged the door shut with her foot. She took a deep cleansing breath. Molly pushed her cold nose into her hand in puppyish delight as Daria scratched all her good spots. Daria smiled as she slowly relaxed. The tension slowly drained from her. *It had been a long shift at the Metro ICU, but well worth it.*

Sunshine chased dissipating storm clouds across the clearing sky and played an errant game of hide-and-seek amongst the trees. Daria took a breath; she filled her lungs with the clean crisp air kissed with a tantalizing hint of sea salt. With a relaxed smile, she soaked in the welcoming ambiance. With her doggy smile, Molly trotted around the corner. The shepherd shook her head playfully. Her leash dangled from her mouth as her dancing dog tags rang out a merry melody. As Molly rushed toward her, Daria felt the remaining tension drain from her in a welcome rush. "Feel like a good long walk, girl? Are you going to drag me through hedges and chase squirrels?"

Molly whined in anticipation, tail wagging madly in a mini cyclone. The big dog danced in place. Daria felt a bone-deep certainty. *Ah...it's good to be home. Life doesn't get much better than this.*

* * *

Kairn stared at the stars coming into focus as they exited the wormhole. The vision had changed. That female was there again. She had been playing with that large canine creature as they ran along a rocky trail. Her laughter had trailed behind her.

His hearts racing, Kairn shivered with remembered pleasure. *I would know that laugh anywhere.*

Kairn stifled his urge to order Darzik to increase the Guardian's speed. *We are already making unusually good time. Our engines are in excellent shape— better than that knowing Breis.*

Kairn felt his fine, short fur ripple involuntarily as a surge of unfamiliar emotion surged through him. Talons extending involuntarily from his fingers with a crisp snick, he finally remembered.

His hearts racing in hope, Kairn savored the rightness of her name. *Her name is Daria.*

He sensed that she was happy. And safe...for now. Kairn felt an unreasonable certainty that she was somewhere on that planet—the one they were straining so hard to reach before the Ichori made irreversible violent, murderous contact. His hearts shifting into a hard fast rhythm, his instincts flared wildly. *MINE! Protect!*

CHAPTER THREE

Kairn snarled. The Guardian had nearly burnt out her ion engines in her frantic race to reach the world now sorely besieged. The GUARDIAN's plasma cannons charged, raking the shields of the massive Ichori warship mercilessly in a relentless barrage.

Additional ships of the Alliance battle group exited the jump into the system. Bringing their weapons to bear, they quickly engaged the Ichori—adding their formidable firepower to the fight.

Kairn grimaced with hearts-felt empathy. *That once beautiful planet.*

Even from their position above their atmosphere, he could see the still smoldering devastation left by the Ichori fusion ordinance. The Ichori had targeted large populated areas. Fires fueled by the Ichori white phosphorus clean-up missiles still burned—destroying everything they came into contact with. The flames poured toxic smoke into the atmosphere, generating storms of acid rain. Wide swathes of the planet were now rendered uninhabitable without extensive reclamation efforts...and the bombs were still dropping.

Alliance ships were built for speed; they wove deftly through the Ichori, scoring multiple hits and wearing down the dense shielding. The Ichori warship did not retreat under the withering fire.

Kairn narrowed his eyes in dawning surprise. Curiosity niggled at him. Despite the Ichori warship's considerable armament, only sporadic enemy fire impacted the Guardian's shields and was easily dispelled.

Fifteen Ichori harvester ships were focusing their transport beams on the planet's huge bodies of water. The generated vortex was greedily suctioning up countless volumes of the precious liquid—their primary objective.

A stray plasma barrage caught a slow-moving harvester retreating, likely replete with water. It exploded in a spectacular ball of flame and steam. Kairn stifled a growl. "Open channel to the fleet."

He snapped, "Have a care when you pick your targets. Try not to catch the harvesters with collateral fire. They are poorly shielded. Even slow as they are, the Ichori know we will not target them. They have an advantage there. The Ichori know we will try to capture them intact. This planet will need all the water we can salvage."

Kairn sighed heavily. "Weapons control, target the armory of the Ichori warship. We need to cripple her before the Ichori initiate a wormhole. Engineering, set coordinates to sensor readings."

His crew grimaced as one. That would likely mean no survivors on the Ichori ship. The Ichori designed their ships with the diabolical placement of their life support adjacent to their armory. They gambled on the reluctance of Alliance ships to incinerate entire crews.

The Ichori had indiscriminately pillaged priceless natural resources from countless systems, leaving a trail of ravaged worlds and dying civilizations in their wake. They had an infernal ability to identify their victims; their reconnaissance was relentless in finding planets which could not mount any defense to speak of.

The bridge crew swore viciously when, one after another, all but five of the remaining harvester drones vanished through an activated wormhole. Just as the wormhole closed—too quickly to track their destination—bombardment from the Alliance fleet penetrated the Ichori warship's shields.

The anti-climactic breaking apart of the Ichori ship brought Kairn no comfort. The warship was just a decoy; it was cannon fodder to allow the drones time to complete their mission. Despite the valiant efforts of the Alliance battle group, the Ichori had succeeded in raping another world of an irreplaceable resource.

Kairn straightened his shoulders. "Darzik, organize triage and SAR teams. Update our translators with this planet's languages. We need to contact whatever government is still in place. We do not want them to think we are the enemy when we make landfall."

Kairn let out a deep breath. "Engineering...Breis, report. Did you retrieve the packages?"

CHAPTER FOUR

Daria shook her head in disbelief. "Mass casualties in the ER. All available medical staff report to the hospital."

The call had come through her landline just before the line went out. Seaside was a small sleepy hamlet comfortably outside the city. It was nestled snugly along the picturesque and very sheer cliffs of the coastline. It would take a while to negotiate the curvy road into the city.

She threw a few changes of comfortable clothes, toiletries, and Molly's favorite toys haphazardly into an overnight bag. "It's all hands on deck, girl. We've got to get to the hospital. I'll keep you in my office."

Daria tucked the bag neatly in the convenient space left between the cases of water and packs of toilet paper piled in the trunk that she kept forgetting to put away.

Daria shrugged ruefully. "For once, maybe it's a good thing I'm such a pack rat."

Molly whined uneasily. Daria turned to her dog, who was pacing anxiously along the cliff behind the cottage. "C'mon, girl. We're in a hurry."

She took a few steps towards the cliff. Daria's voice trailed off.

The wind sloughed through the tree branches. The air felt different, smelled different. It was too quiet. Too dry. Too warm. With a sinking heart, Daria joined Molly. They stared out at the vast, barren plain stretching to the horizon strewn with dying kelp forests where the mighty Pacific Ocean had crashed over the rocky coastline the day before.

* * *

The Next Day

The alarms on the ventilators sounded repeatedly despite frequent adjustments at bedside. The woman's lungs were stiff and unable to exchange oxygen on maximal levels of oxygen and high levels of pressure.

The woman was heavily sedated and paralyzed in an attempt to minimize her oxygen needs. A team of nurses painstakingly turned the woman onto her stomach, the respiratory therapist with a hand glued to the breathing tube keeping their fragile patient alive.

There was a collective sigh of tentative relief as the team carefully settled the woman back onto the bed. Daria adjusted the ventilator again and watched with relief as the red flashing numbers slowly climbed into acceptable green territory.

Daria traded a long look with Emily, her best friend and a badass ICU nurse. Daria rested her hand gently on the patient's prone upper body. She murmured reassuringly, "Maggie, my name is Daria. I'm sorry. I know you're scared. You're in the intensive care unit. I'll be helping take care of you. We've got a good team working with you. Keep up the hard work. You're doing a little better."

Daria's eyes flicked to Maggie's monitor. The woman's vital signs had spiked. "We're going to give you some more medicine to help you relax. You can't move because we had to give you medicine to decrease your oxygen needs. You can't talk because you have a breathing tube in your airway. That pressure you feel is the machine...your ventilator breathing for you. Hang in there. Small baby steps."

Daria spoke quietly to Emily. "Maggie needs more sedation. Give her a 3 mg bolus of Versed and increase her drip to 6 mg per hour. Bolus another 100 micrograms of Fentanyl and titrate her Fentanyl drip as well. Those burns and fractures have got to hurt. She needs to not fight the vent so she can heal. We'll add Ketamine if we have to."

Daria paused, thinking a moment. "Have wound care and plastics see her as well."

Vent alarms shrilled in the next room. Daria couldn't remember how long she had been in the ICU. It was "all hands on deck." They were all running on caffeine and adrenaline.

The ICU was stretched beyond their limit with burn, crush, and inhalational injury victims. Overflowing into step down units. They weren't a certified trauma center, but they were serving as one now. There were so many crush injuries. The number of available vents was running perilously low.

Priority was triage and stabilization. Electricity was out. The overhead lights flickered yet again. Daria could hear the collective sigh of relief around the unit at the quiet reassuring hum of the generators. They were only running on generator power now. Cell service and the internet were down. She pushed sweat-dampened bangs off her forehead. The lights dimmed momentarily before they steadied. Daria leaned forward, stretching out the nagging ache building in her back. *Thank God the ventilators have back-up batteries.*

Rumors were circulating about a gas leak in the city. Was it earthquakes? They'd all heard the explosions. One after another. And then they just stopped.

Where had the ocean gone? And what could have caused it? Wild rumors were running rampant. The latest top conspiracy theory was little green men.

Daria snorted. At this point, she didn't know and really didn't care. She had a unit full of critical patients, a shorthanded and overworked staff. She gave thanks again for the dedicated doctors and nurses she worked with. Mentally, she chanted again. *We're not done yet. Almost there. One day at a time. Keep your head in the game...triage and stabilization.*

Daria rubbed stiff muscles in her neck and felt a fine tremor in her fingers. They were all here for the duration, however long that would be. It was a good thing she hadn't yet left for her vacation a good 3 hours upstate when the disaster sirens sounded and the emergency call came through.

Danny, the X-ray tech, pulled up the film. The tubes and lines looked good. The lung damage was, for now, holding stable. The team traded warily hopeful smiles.

Daria reviewed the patient's blood work. She reminded herself. *She has a name. It's Maggie.*

Emily silently passed Daria a cup of lukewarm coffee. The nurse took a deep breath. "How was the drive in?"

With a smile of thanks, Daria drained the bitter brew in several large gulps. Daria replied absently as she quickly wrote holding orders. "The coast roads were fine. There's a huge amount of structural damage to the city."

Emily sighed. "Remember 9/11. All those ERs and not nearly as many patients as they hoped for."

Looking up at that, Daria grimaced. "God willing...this time, there will be survivors."

Daria swallowed hard, hanging on to hope. "We're going to get a lot of casualties. I don't think any of us are going home for a while."

Emily mutely passed over the latest critical results that the lab had called up. Daria frowned. "Type and cross for 4 units. Put a page out for Dr. Larsen."

Emily replied dully. "No one's seen him...and the paging system is down."

Daria barked out sharply, "Put a call out over the PA."

Daria fell silent, remembering her friend. They had started at the hospital together. *I hope he and Laura are OK.*

Emily spoke quietly, "Daria."

No response. More loudly, Emily said, "Dr. Morrissey, the woman in room 28 is dropping her O2 stats."

Daria managed a weary smile. "Stellar job here, people. Keep it up. I'm headed to 28 next."

CHAPTER FIVE

Lupera was a warrior planet. Her Clans excelled as defenders in the Alliance. Soldiers followed orders. But these...His claws cut grooves into his desk as he re-read the Guardian's orders to set course immediately for Centauri Station for repairs.

Kairn shook his head sharply, trying to subdue the growl rising in his throat. He bit back expletives. "Large areas of the planet have lost their source of energy. Their large bodies of Water, particularly those with salinity, have been depleted by more than 60%. Their atmosphere has been contaminated by the toxic smoke generated by the Ichori bombardment."

Kairn shook his head as he listed the planet's many woes. "I have sent triage teams to the planet surface. They have made contact with the rudimentary authorities."

Kirov, the Guardian's chief Medico, added quietly, "The humanoids on the planet are understandably wary but have accepted our help. Temperatures are rising. Communications and transportation has been disrupted. The population has sustained large number of casualties. They do not have the resources to survive the fallout from the Ichori attack."

The Alliance Alpha sighed heavily and glared.

Kairn continued grimly. "Luperan honor dictates we stay to offer whatever aid we can. The Guardian did not sustain serious damage. My crew can manage the repairs well enough. Without our immediate and sustained assistance, this is an extinction level event for this planet."

The Alpha flashed his fangs and grunted. "The Guardian is best equipped to track the Ichori drones and identify their base. Maybe even their next target, but...your point about this planet is well taken."

The Alpha nodded his head. "We understand honor. We cannot leave this planet to her own devices. She does not have the resources or a unified government to recover from this. Permission granted."

The Council leader leaned forward intently. "Supplies en route. Establish contact with what is left of their government."

The Alpha's mask lifted, his shrewd eyes suddenly lighting with humor. "You are driving this. Captain Kairn, I am appointing you as Ambassador to this unfortunate planet. Even after what she has suffered, this world..."

The Alpha consulted the report. "This...Earth is still blessed with an abundance of natural resources. I entrust her to your care. You will help her repair her infrastructure. Do what you can to preserve—even recover anything salvageable from her resources. I know you will not exploit her vulnerability. Unlike some of your less savory peers, I know I can rely on you to do what is right. I know how you detest political gamesmanship."

Kairn managed not to roll his eyes. His old commander was a wily old bastard whose ultimate priority was the safety of his crew. A master of strategy. Kairn's ruff prickled in wary suspicion. He remembered his former commander's sometimes twisted sense of humor. A sly grin flickered on the Alpha's stern mouth.

Kairn frowned. "Recon reports a sizable number of warring factions."

Perusing the reports, he added, "They are a primitive world without a global leadership."

Professional mask back in place, the Alpha leaned forward. "What did you retrieve from the Ichori warship? Any actionable intelligence to identify their next target?"

His eyes narrowing thoughtfully, Kairn ran sharp claws through his thick ruff. He frowned, "Not what, but whom. We thought we would transport more, but the entire Ichori ship was crewed by drones and a skeleton crew. Their captain is cooperating."

Kairn's eyes warmed with empathy. "By the size of their ship, we estimate he lost nearly the entirety of his crew in their assault on the planet. We were only able to transport five off the bridge. Darzik is in charge of their interrogation."

The Alpha smiled slowly in appreciation. "Your science officer? He was promoted to XO. I have heard of him. Interesting choice..."

CHAPTER SIX

Kairn perused the impressive compilation of reports. His crew was doing an exemplary job with the captured harvesters.

The recon team had boarded the massive transports with minimal damage to their structure and defanged their token automated defenses.

On the fly, Darzik had re-written self-destruct sequences which had been set to trigger when the ships did not enter the wormhole.

Kairn never understood how they could bring themselves to do it, but standard Ichori protocol dictated the scuttling of any ships they did not recover. Their rulers and generals were notoriously indifferent to the wanton waste of lives and resources, even (perhaps especially) those of their own people.

Engineering was meticulously manipulating the slow, clumsy controls of the harvesters. They coordinated the careful return of countless tons of water to the oceans of Earth with as much alacrity as safety margins allowed.

Engineering was being kept extremely busy. Breis and his teams were also charged with purifying the atmosphere of the toxins generated by the fires—which were finally, by the grace of the Gods, under control.

Kairn nodded with justifiable pride in his crew. The SAR teams had recovered many survivors from the rubble of the countless leveled buildings. Kirov and his Medico team were stretched thin with the (thankfully) high demand for their expertise.

In their copious spare time, Breis was trying to get the Guardian's simulators to produce much-needed cryogen tanks and wands for the planet's overwhelmed hospital systems. Kairn narrowed his eyes. *This is a top priority: We need to assess the intrinsic capabilities of Earth's medical cadre and familiarize them with their new tech.*

Kairn smiled slightly. The assembled disgruntled crowd fell into an uneasy silence at the sight of his sharp canines. Kairn mused consideringly. This planet has had many insightful souls. *One of my favorites, a Maimonides, had advised, "Give a man a fish, you feed him for a day. Teach him to fish, he will feed himself for a lifetime."*

With a carefully impassive glance at the dissatisfied crowd, Kairn nodded to himself. *Interesting visual. It is sage advice indeed, but I doubt it will be received well.*

Kairn drew in a long deep breath, struggling to maintain his calm. He surveyed the restive audience he had the dubious honor of addressing. He recognized the avid avarice in the many faces. The Earthlings...

Kairn corrected himself. *They like being called humans. I must do better at remembering that.*

The large, raucous crowd jockeyed for position, shoving each other out of the way aggressively.

As Kairn calmly summarized the salient points, he was interrupted repeatedly.

"The suspicious lack of speed..."

"The arbitrary sites being selected..."

These were the more polite of the belligerent accusations being hurled at him and his crew. It was fast becoming the rallying cry of the illogical mob before him.

Kairn could not understand these beings. Their planet and what was left of their civilization was still reeling from the Ichori attack. They were allegedly sentient. Kairn raised a disappointed brow as they argued contentiously amongst themselves. Without any compunction, they jockeyed shamelessly for coveted positions of power in their new world government.

His escalating snarl drew their attention. Kairn bristled briefly before regaining his composure. "As Ambassador to your planet, I can reassure you that the Alliance has no plans to annex your planet or claim her as a colony. The Guardian is..."

Someone shouted from the back, "You brought this evil here. How do we know this wasn't your great plan all along?"

A strident nasal voice chimed in belligerently, grating on his sensitive ears. "What about your ship? Why is it still here? Why are your alien crew running around? You silver ones are acceptable, but we have no use for fraternization with the rest of your like. Especially those big black and red ones!"

An appalled silence fell over the humans. Guilt flashed in hurriedly downcast eyes, yet not one of them spoke up to refute the ugly words or to chastise, let alone condemn the prejudiced speakers spewing the hateful vitriol. Their feet shifted uneasily. The fluorescent lights highlighted the sweat beginning to bead on their foreheads.

Kairn saw Darzik towering over the human security squad at the side of the room. His black ruff began to stiffen in outrage. Kairn shook his head very slightly; his ruff slowly relaxing, Darzik settled reluctantly.

Kairn drew a deep cleansing breath and found a thin semblance of civility. His voice had dropped several octaves. With commendable control, Kairn stated, "Black. Bronze. Grey. Silver. Red. White. Blue. All the shades between. You will find all of them among my crew. Color is genetics. It does not denote any particular position or gift. My crew earned their position on my ship based on merit and character."

His voice softened slightly with dawning pity. "I had thought you did the same."

His eyes hardened. His words fell like stones into the stillness. "Let me be clear. The Guardian is here to aid in your recovery. We will serve as your shield until such time that you can protect yourselves. It is our fervent hope that Earth will, one day, be a valued member in the Alliance."

He continued, emotions coloring his voice. "A strong partnership must have trust between us. I see now this is not possible with you. I have no use for your sort who sees this attack as an opportunity to profit off the misery of your brothers and sisters. To discriminate because of color?"

Kairn shook his head with sorrowful gravity. "I hope that your sorry lot is the dregs of humanity. The Water will go where it must to do the best for the stability of your planet. It saddens me greatly that you choose not to recognize that. We will not have any further dealings with you!"

A curt nod at Darzik sent his security detail to escort the loudly protesting rabble summarily from the council chamber.

After the room emptied of the still squabbling humans, Kairn rumbled in frustration, "Thus far, these negotiations are not promising."

Darzik laughed shortly. "That was quite an understatement."

His XO snorted. "You were very articulate. Quite the diplomat. And far kinder than I would be. I think this lot is well beyond salvaging."

Kairn snorted, flicking a tall ear in succinct response. He stared out the window, watching his crew efficiently unload the medical tech earmarked for human hospitals. He noted the many small human volunteers.

Initially cautious around the Luperans, they—with only a brief understandable pause—were now swarming his base camp. They were actually trying to assist his crew. Kairn considered them thoughtfully.

Their trepidation was understandable as my crew towers over them. I admit I find the short duration very commendable.

With a widening smile, Kairn reminded himself aloud, "Give a man a fish, you feed him for a day. Teach him to fish, he will feed himself for a lifetime."

Darzik stared at him a moment. His XO barked out a sharp laugh. "I understand the sentiment, but I do not think it applies here."

Kairn laughed quietly. "Not with the lot you just escorted out, but I think you underestimate humans, brother."

He gestured at the many Luperans who had grown determined human shadows. "These humans have a steep learning curve. I think we will be quite impressed by their commitment."

Darzik joined him at the window, his large ears swiveling forward intently. With a lilt of surprise in his voice, he answered thoughtfully, "I hope they prove me wrong."

Kairn felt his hackles and ruff stiffen in quiet controlled frustration. "These meetings have been a waste of time. Our problem is that we have been dealing with career politicians. Self-serving and short sighted."

Kairn shook his head with a slow smile. "Find me humans with honor. Those involved in the evacuation will be those of sounder character. Look amongst them."

Darzik nodded briskly. He snapped out a smart salute. "Wise recommendation...Ambassador."

Kairn cuffed his XO and old friend lightly. "Insubordination is not tolerated."

Darzik grinned. "I was impressed. I did not know you had such a gift for diplomacy."

Kairn grimaced. "Perish the thought. I am a simple ship's captain... and I wish to stay that way."

Darzik shook his head, his grin widening. "Famous last words. Keep reminding yourself of that short-lived fact, Ambassador."

Darzik started making notes and recommendations on his comm. Kairn's voice roughened with an impatient growl. He would have to address and correct the putrid abyss that was currently human leadership...then he could search for his female. *At least, I can feel in my hearts that she is safe.*

He moved onto another worrisome topic. "How goes the questioning of the Ichori crew? They are Alliance prisoners of war...and will be accorded standard courtesy as such."

Darzik nodded shortly. "About that. You met them when we transported them aboard. They are in bad shape. It is obvious that their injuries are not from the battle. The wounds look like those we would see in prisoners of war...torture survivors. They spoke up voluntarily."

Darzik rubbed his large ears with a pained grimace. "My vow, Kairn. I heard only the truth...and a great deal of turmoil and pain. The captain says they are key members of a burgeoning resistance movement. Their goal is to topple the corrupt Ichori ruling family. Amongst their number, they claim that they count most of the Ichori officers on fleet ships particularly in the Ichori elite reconnaissance group."

At Kairn's disbelieving silent stare, Darzik nodded slowly. "The captain swears that they were brutally interrogated by Ichori government types."

With a snort, Darzik grimaced. "A euphemism for torture. When they would not disclose remaining resistance members, they were imprisoned on the bridge of that warship with controls locked on auto pilot. Someone wanted to ensure they had a good view of their approaching demise."

Darzik growled deep in his throat. "Their ship was programmed to self-destruct after harvesting the planet's water and transporting it back to the Ichori Empire."

Darzik heard Kairn's claws extend with a crisp snick. His eyes darkening, Kairn growled. "If they share anything like the camaraderie of our bridge crew, being rendered helpless and making them watch each other die would be the ultimate torture. That is masochistic and diabolical—and the act of a sociopathic monster."

The XO continued his report grimly. "I can understand the twisted logic. The Ichori people get their war heroes. The government gets propaganda for their unsuspecting masses. At the same time, they rid themselves of a core of the resistance before the movement can take root. If it had gone according to their plan, they could have broken the back—the spirit—of the resistance. Multiple targets with one projectile in one fell swoop."

Darzik straightened his shoulders. "That Ichori captain looked me in the eye the entire time. His only concern was for his surviving crew."

Darzik paused. He added solemnly, "Kairn...brother...he reminds me of you. I believe him."

Silence fell as the two seasoned combat veterans stared at each other. If this was indeed true, this could change everything as they knew it.

CHAPTER SEVEN

Daria woke when the shouts penetrated her deep sleep. She brushed haphazardly at her wrinkled scrubs. She stretched gingerly—wincing at her stiff muscles. Daria joined the other curious hospital staff crowding the narrow hallway. She rubbed sleep from her eyes and peered down the hall. She couldn't see much over the tightly-packed bodies. She yawned loudly. Her voice hoarse, she muttered absently, "What's all the excitement about? Is there a code somewhere?"

Daria frowned, now more awake. "Where is it?"

Emily slanted a look at her, a wry smile tugging at her lips. Emily gave Daria a gentle hip bump. "Dial it down a notch, tiger. We're doing well for now. But, remember the rumor about little green men? You've got to take a look at them. They're not green and sure not little! They're going to give you palpitations. They're pure eye candy!"

* * *

Kairn pointed out key areas on the hologram. "This is the mobile triage area with our Medicos—they are what we call physicians. They have portable cryogen tanks, which can stabilize injuries. Those who need more aggressive treatment can be transferred to our ship."

Kairn looked around the room at the many interested faces listening to him. He nodded with approval. "These machines control the ambient temperature and convert excess carbon dioxide to Water. They also neutralize pollutants and acids contaminating the atmosphere. We have enough to supply major cities and are awaiting transport of more."

The human administrator nodded as he stared at the hologram. The door opened quietly. His gaze still fixed on the hologram, the administrator gestured absently. "We appreciate everything. Frankly, we need all the help we can get. Our resources are stretched...strained beyond our limits."

The older human male smiled. His face was etched with fatigue, but his smile was sincere. The administrator ran a hand through his rumpled thinning hair. "I know you have limited time, but I asked the heads of my Emergency Room and ICU to join us. They will know best where your resources can do the most good. These are dedicated physicians and nurses. They can identify any incoming critical cases who need more care than we can provide."

An elusive, sweetly-spiced fragrance subtly graced the still air. His hearts stuttered then lurched into joyful determined life. Kairn took a deep breath, his hearts settling into a thrumming rhythm. Kairn could feel his eyes start to glow and his fangs lengthen.

He turned, staring at the ragged line of tired, rumpled humans gathered at the narrow entrance. Impatience surged as they trailed in. They stopped in front of him. They were not military per se; yet, to a one, he could see the dedication and discipline in their eyes.

He gave a respectful nod to the first human, a male. Trying not to be overtly rude, Kairn drew a deep breath and felt that same scent dance tantalizingly over his sensitive nose. Dizzying certainty soothed his shocked and disbelieving soul with a sense of wonder and hope. In rapt silence, Kairn stared at the adorably rumpled female human standing quietly in front of him. She was his dream made flesh and bone. *My Daria...She was here all along.*

Daria stared at the HUGE aliens. They towered over the people in the room. Her thoughts raced. *Looming over all the people in the room.*

Bipedal. Humanoid. The requisite number of eyes and ears. Remember, they're NOT human. These numbers don't apply. Very deep-set eyes. Tall, pointed tufted ears...and they rotate! A prominent high-bridged nose. I'm being unforgivably rude. I'm staring. I need to stop. What's wrong with me? They've done so much already. Dear Lord, I'm still staring.

Daria had the overwhelming sense of a wolf pack on the hunt. Daria tried to subdue her unruly thoughts. She made a concerted effort and shifted her gaze to the hologram. They were all impressive, but she kept finding her eyes returning to the leader.

The bass tones of his voice sank into her bones. His amber eyes abruptly fixed on her. With a start, Daria saw his variegated silver hair on his head and the fine fur across his shoulders ripple as if in a nonexistent breeze.

* * *

Kairn sent another gentle mental nudge toward his Mate. Still no response.

"Ambassador Kairn of the Guardian, these are some of our best. This is Dr. Watkins in the ER."

Kairn absently acknowledged the introduction. The administrator continued, "...and Dr. Darianna Morrissey and charge nurse Emily Garrison in ICU."

All of his attention centered on the petite female. Daria. Her name settled sweetly in his hearts. She said quietly and surely, "Daria, please. I'm so glad to meet you. We would have lost so many more without your help."

His ears rotated and stiffened, brushing the ceiling. His female extended a hand with a shy smile. Kairn accepted her hand, noting the fine tremors indicative of fatigue. Mindful of his claws, he retracted them quickly. He cradled her small hand gently in his massive one, marveling at the contrast in size and strength.

Kairn felt pride rise at her insightful passionate questions. He sent her subtle waves of affection and support. Setting his jaw, he tamped down the surging crest of hunger spiking his blood.

Wonder surged brightly through him. *My* female.

Correcting himself, Kairn made a mental note again. *Her name is Daria.*

A long yawn made her pause her inquisitive questions. Kairn watched a sudden rise of rosy color wash over her features.

Kairn rumbled abruptly, "We are done for today and will evaluate progress tomorrow."

His spirit soaring, Kairn ignored the startled look Darzik sent him.

CHAPTER EIGHT

Daria

Emily murmured under her breath. "Those are some tall drinks of water."

Daria shook her head with a soft laugh and started down the hall alone toward her office. She sensed something and turned to find that same silver-furred alien moving to her side. Bowing slightly, he extended his arm in endearing old-world courtesy.

Daria paused before she rested her fingers on it. The short layer of decadently silky fur tickled the sensitive skin of her palm. Daria barely resisted her sudden urge to trace patterns on his temptingly warm skin. Her fingers twitched slightly in a subtle but noticeable movement. Under her touch, Daria felt his muscles tighten and then relax in slow delicious degrees.

They walked in companionable silence. The alien radiated extraordinary heat. Her thoughts raced. *My alien...*

Daria shook her head slightly. She worried about her lower lip as she corrected herself. *Not mine. The alien is beautiful.*

Daria took in a slow breath. *No...That still wasn't right. It's too tame. He is too alive...too masculine...too intensely focused...*

Lost in the rabbit's hole of her thoughts, Daria found herself outside her office. She could hear enthusiastic scratching as Molly pawed insistently inside at the door. The scratching paused abruptly. A chorus of eager whine and yips sounded.

Daria spoke quickly. "That's my dog, Molly. I don't know how she'll be around..."

Her voice trailed off as his full lips parted, flashing very large...very sharp...teeth. *Good Lord. Was that his smile?*

Daria felt a tendril of unfamiliar heat uncurl low in her belly. She hid a delicate shiver. *Whoa...that's not fear. That felt so good.*

Daria licked her suddenly dry lips. She saw his gaze drop to her lips for a heated moment. With a barely perceptible pause, he lifted his gaze. His smile widened as he gestured for her to open the door.

As she opened the door a sliver, Molly shouldered her way roughly out of the room with a challenging growl. Daria groaned. *Why did I do that? I'll be the cause of an intergalactic incident. What was I thinking?*

Daria grabbed for Molly's collar but narrowly missed. The alien dropped to his knees in a smooth motion. He stared at Molly, a sub vocal sound subtly vibrating the air. Molly sat slowly with her head tilted attentively as she listened. After long, quiet moments, her tail started to wave slowly. The big shepherd let out a quizzical whine.

The alien rose gracefully. He towered over Daria, easily two to three feet taller. Daria felt her heart flutter. With a sense of dawning wonder, she realized in a dizzying rush. *I don't feel threatened. I feel safe... protected...cherished.*

The alien's smile widened. "I am..."

He paused. "Please call me Kairn. If you will accept me, I need to know you."

Daria frowned slightly. *Accept him? He couldn't mean that. It must be a glitch in the translator...*

Before she could ask the question, his eyes began to glow. Raising a huge finely molded hand, he carefully brushed her hair back. He took a slow deep breath.

She no longer found his smile intimidating as his expression warmed. "You don't need to ask. It is not the translator. Those are my chosen words for you."

Daria felt herself relax in slow increments at his easy, undemanding manner. She could feel herself smile back. Her eyes lingered on his lips just a fraction too long. Daria could feel her cheeks heat with a blush. *Now that I know that's what it is, I really like his smile.*

She glanced up, meeting the alien's bright amber gaze. Daria checked herself. *His name is Kairn.*

Kairn's eyes seemed to glow. He studied her face carefully. His deep voice rumbled pleasantly. "Tell me of you, Daria."

His voice lingered over her name. His smile widened as she began to speak. He listened intently as his head tilted toward her. Daria felt a delicious shiver tease her spine. *It's heady stuff...being the sole focus of his attention.*

Daria continued talking...about her job...about Molly...about her snug little cabin in the woods. While she spoke, she reminded herself, *Kairn is the Ambassador. He's probably just being polite. He's a gorgeous alien who's being kind to his guide. Don't go reading too much into this. Remember...*

Daria groaned out a rueful, wistful laugh. *This is real life...not a book ...or a movie.*

Even as she chided herself, Daria couldn't help remembering the way she had felt all through her accelerated, abbreviated high school and college years: *Always looking from the outside in.*

Daria glanced up...way up into Kairn's attentive face. *I'm not sure, but he sure seems to be fascinated with...something...or someone.*

His intense focus did not waver from her. His amber eyes lightened, alive with unmistakable heated interest.

Kairn tilted his head, drifting infinitesimally closer. His gaze dipped very briefly to her lips before locking warmly with her eyes.

Kairn's smile widened, warming even more. He crooked his elbow in gentle invitation. "Please walk with me. Show me your world."

Daria stared at his proffered arm. She lay her hand lightly on his arm. The thick muscles contracted under her diffident touch. Kairn looked at her intently with an unspoken tacit question.

Daria nodded, shyness painting her cheeks a warm rose. Kairn tucked her hand in closer. She glanced up, getting lost in the warm welcome in his gaze. Her fingers tightened instinctively. Kairn's smile deepened even more.

They walked down the hall. Molly barked happily, gamboling around them. Kairn watched her antics with an affectionate smile. Daria relaxed and took her time. Kairn automatically adjusted his stride to accommodate her much shorter legs. Sunlight streaming through the window warmed her face and limned Kairn in a soft nimbus of silver.

Daria could feel an ember of hope flicker to life. *Is this real? If this is a dream, I don't care...but I don't want to wake up. I never believed in love at first sight, but there is something special between us. He feels it too. Somehow... with Kairn, I don't feel alone anymore.*

CHAPTER NINE

A Short Time Later: Daria

The restoration of Earth was a painstaking but rewarding process. Daria and Kairn had managed to make time for each other nearly every day.

After her shift in the ICU, Kairn would find her—serving as her guard and companion whenever his demanding duties as dual captain and Ambassador allowed.

They would spend whatever time they had in long talks about the Earth...restoration efforts...the foibles of old Earth politics...Molly...her friends...his crew whom he saw as brothers...her cabin. In short, they talked about everything...and anything.

Daria could see the tension of the day drain from Kairn with each precious visit. Over time, they built a solid foundation of a true friendship, nurturing a deepening bond she dared not give a name to. The tantalizing hint of more shimmered between them with a scintillating, ever-growing, tangible chemistry

Today was going to be a busy, rewarding day for them both. She had not caught a glimpse of Kairn. The Guardian had deployed another fleet of atmospheric scrubbers to neutralize and collect the residual toxic particulates left by the Ichori attack.

Until they had built more units, the Luperans had been transporting the most critically injured to their Command Base—even the Guardian when necessary. Their Medicos were now welcome, familiar faces in the busiest ICUs.

The Luperans had built and given Earth several hundred portable cryogen wands and a hundred of the full-size cryogen units distributed to the areas they were most needed—with more on the way.

Their ICU was the lucky recipient of two fully operational cryogen units. Daria shook her head sadly. *Translation: we have a lot of high acuity patients...even this far out.*

Kairn had arranged for Kirov, the Guardian's Medico, to demonstrate its use to the excited human medical personnel. They were doing rounds in the trauma ICU. Daria counted herself lucky to be among the select group.

The priceless gift of the new tech was evident in the dramatically improving condition of patient after critically ill patient. Daria felt her eyes burn with overwhelming relief.

She smiled widely as she recognized Nils Larsen. He was still pale but recovering well. He and Laura had been trapped in the rubble. A Luperan SAR team had dug them out. They had both spent time in the cryogen tanks and were enthusiastic and vocal living proof of the tech's nigh miraculous capabilities.

Nils glanced up, his eyes warming as he smiled. As Daria looked around, she could see understanding and gratitude dawn on the faces of the exhausted medical staff crowding around the bed.

Except...One of the visiting physicians was a tall, svelte blonde. Her entire attention was focused on exploring the admittedly impressive physical attributes of the Luperan Medico. With commendable discipline, Kirov studiously ignored her blatant overtures with controlled composure and a barely discernible chilly distaste.

Felicia had the sleek, barely-there curves and carriage of a supermodel. She dressed in designer figure-hugging dresses and sky-high Louboutin stiletto heels. You always knew where she'd been by the dizzying cloud of perfume trailing behind her.

When Felicia leaned over, she flashed everyone an embarrassingly long look at her cleavage. Her hem climbed northward of mid-thigh, barely covering her privates. Daria looked away hastily on the high likelihood that Felicia was going commando. Daria grimaced. *There are some things you just can't unsee. As much as I'd want to, I can't really bleach my brain!*

Daria turned her head away to hide her amused expression. *I suspect I have more material in my T-shirt than that woman has in her entire outfit.*

Daria walked away. *I sure hope Felicia doesn't develop pneumonia. I bet five pounds of Godiva dark chocolate that Felicia would be a demanding nightmare as a patient...Hell...that's not a bet. It's a total Gimme.*

Daria took a cautious sniff and wrinkled her nose at the heavy floral perfume. *Good Lord, if there was any static electricity, Felicia and anyone within twenty-five feet of her would be engulfed in flames.*

Daria shook her head. *Oops...whoa...where did that come from? That was catty!*

Daria grimaced at the accidental pun. *Ouch.*

Emily elbowed her with an appreciative grin. "I didn't know you had that in you, chica."

Daria groaned as she flushed slightly. "I said that aloud, didn't I?"

Daria grimaced, then smiled ruefully. "I didn't mean to say that."

Emily shrugged. "It's just me...and besides...it's true."

Daria actually didn't care that Felicia looked like a runway model and flirted outrageously with all the men there. *What bothers me is that Felicia didn't pay any attention to the instructions for use of the cryogen tech. She doesn't give a rat's ass about the opportunity any dedicated physician would have treasured.*

Daria snorted derisively. *She also took every opportunity (engineering quite a few) to touch the male medical personnel—focusing on an overtly uncomfortable Kirov.*

The other doctors and nurses worked around an oblivious Felicia with distaste. It was sadly very obvious to all that Felicia didn't give a damn about the medicine...and therefore her patients.

Daria could easily tell that Kirov was an excellent medical officer. He had excellent clinical judgement and a supportive bedside manner. His tolerance, however, for poorly thought-out questions was basically zero. Kirov also telegraphed a blatant need for a very generous personal space—which meant he despised Felicia with a thinly disguised passion.

Daria grinned. *I like him already.*

Kairn walked in toward the end of the tutorial workshop. His warm eyes scanned the sea of humans, searching intently for and finding hers across the room.

Kairn stopped briefly to speak with Kirov. Daria had spent enough time with Kairn. She recognized the subtle Luperan version of a pained grimace on Kirov's face.

Kairn listened intently and shook his head sharply. Daria saw his grin as he thumped Kirov on his shoulders. With a growing smile, Kairn started across the room toward her.

He nodded politely at humans he knew but did not pause. As he walked past her, Felicia stared at Kairn with sultry come-hither eyes. His eyes warmly set on Daria, Kairn did not notice the flirtatious blonde.

He was several feet away from Daria when Felicia adroitly engineered a bump into his side. Daria fumed. *You cannot accidentally bump into someone of Kairn's size. It's like you walked into the side of a barn!*

Felicia had grabbed onto his massive bicep and had slung her body into his chest. She was clinging to him like a kudzu vine. Daria stared at them. Aware of a sharp stinging in her hands, she winced. Looking down at her hands, she realized that she had inadvertently dug her nails into her palms. Small beads of blood welled up. Emily murmured loudly next to her. "Isn't that the one that ate the South?"

Daria groaned. "Not again! I thought about it...Did I really say that?"

Emily chortled. "Hell yeah. She's sure not subtle. If it's any consolation, he looks like he smelled something bad...nope...make that something dead."

Startled, Daria looked up just in time. Felicia's practiced cloying soprano tone sounded shrill to her ears. "I need help. I twisted my ankle."

Daria growled. She took a step toward Felicia, her hands clenching. Emily put a restraining hand on her shoulder. "Down girl. Don't worry. Your guy's a good one. Trust me. He's got this. Wait for it..."

Kairn stiffened. He halted abruptly and glared at the oblivious woman. Daria watched spellbound...as Kairn found his target with pinpoint accuracy. With only the very tips of his fingers, he dispassionately and painstakingly peeled each of Felicia's long perfectly manicured nails off his arm.

Daria blinked, trying to hide her grin. *Dear God, I've seen people peel off leeches with less disgust.*

Kairn did not attempt to mask his expression of utter distaste. His eyes darkened to a deep bronze. His gaze never drifted below her jaw.

Kairn spoke softly, but his bass tones carried well in the hushed room. "This is a workshop intended for the dedicated health professionals working in the intensive care unit. Your colleagues are dressed in attire appropriate for the hands-on care they provide. I strongly suggest you take a cue from them."

His darkening gaze swept over the rest of the doctors and nurses wearing the standard uniform of scrubs and sneakers. His voice was cold and measured. "Mayhap if you did not wear shoes that made you weave like a drunkard and clothes that hamper your stride, you would not fall as often. I did not invite your touch. Remove yourself from all parts of my body immediately—or I will do it for you. I will only warn you this once. I am *not* available."

Her eyes flickered with poorly concealed alarm. Felicia backed off with an indignant huff. She sniffed as she blustered. "I don't have to stand for this kind of abuse."

Kairn ignored her diatribe as background noise. He flicked a brief glance at Kirov. "The same rule applies to my crew. Without exception, they are off limits."

Kairn turned his back and started toward Daria again. Felicia made a strangled sound in her throat, her voice harsh and loud. "You're turning me down for that?! Well...there's just no accounting for taste, is there?"

Kairn's head turned sharply toward her. Whatever she saw on his face made her voice trail off. Felicia took several shaky steps back. Her pupils dilated and the color drained from her face, leaving it a ghastly white under her makeup.

Kairn's words dropped like stones into the appalled silence. His voice was cold and emotionless. "Never speak like that to my...to her. You are not worthy."

He jerked his head at Kirov. "See to it. She is not welcome here. Not ever again."

Kirov nodded, keeping the shell-shocked Felicia at arm's length. The taciturn medico looked quite gratified as he escorted Felicia out in a hasty and clumsy exit.

Kairn stared after them, glowering darkly until they exited the ICU. Loud clapping and a few whoops of approval broke the tension in the air. Catching her eye, Nils pointed at Kairn with a grin, giving Daria an enthusiastic thumbs-up. Daria rolled her eyes at her old friend. She mouthed. "How's Laura?"

Nils' grin widened as he gave her two enthusiastic thumbs-up. Daria shook her head as the automated doors slid shut with an anticlimactic muffled thud. Daria murmured to Emily. "Laura and Nils are good."

Emily rolled her eyes. "Duh...anyone with eyes can see that."

Emily nudged Daria, musing with an appreciative grin. "Wow..."

Emily drawled out the name. "Fe-liiiii-ciiii-a. There's crashing and burning. And then there's that!"

Daria sighed. "Just goes to show that the dumbest person in the medical school class is still, unfortunately, an MD."

Daria didn't try to hide her wide smile as Kairn finally made his way to her side. He lifted a gentle hand, cupping her cheek in his palm. His amber eyes were brightening to gold. His voice was low and soft. "I apologize if I caused you any embarrassment. It was not my intention. I hope..."

Abruptly, Kairn broke off. Taking in a deep breath, he sniffed at the air.

His eyes darkened to a cold angry brown. Kairn carefully picked up her hands and stared at the indentations and cuts left by her nails. His voice was harsh. "What happened here?"

Daria shrugged helplessly. She couldn't imagine how to start explaining it. Kairn was silent, then lifted her palms to his lips. Ignoring their riveted audience, he kissed each shallow cut with tangible tenderness.

He held her gaze, his eyes again a warm amber shading into gold. He spoke softly, for her ears only. "I regret any pain I have caused you. I am sorry you had to witness that. I promise you...that will never happen again."

Kairn's hand dropped down to tuck her arm gently into the crook of his elbow, nestling her closely into his side. Daria rested her fingers lightly on the hard muscles of his arm. Kairn reached over with his other hand, pressing her hand firmly into his warm flesh.

Daria's voice was soft. She could hear the note of uncertainty in it. He'd been so adamant with Felicia, she needed to be sure. "Is it OK for me to touch you without invitation? You said you weren't available."

Kairn leaned down. She could feel his warm fragrant breath on her face. She felt him bury his nose in her hair and sniff. "Let me clarify. I do not wish any misunderstandings. You are the only one whose touch I invite...that I welcome. I was not available to her."

Kairn's eyes were tender and warm...and glowing. He dropped a light kiss on her hair. "With you, I am. Always."

Kairn added slowly with a proud smile. "I am glad you are possessive of me. As I am of you."

Her cheeks warmed with a shy blush as her fingers stroked possessively over his silky warm fur and even warmer skin. Daria was quiet as she mulled his words. *That felt like a vow.*

In the background, Daria registered Emily excusing herself quickly. Daria snuggled close into Kairn's side and felt his arms circle her in a gentle embrace. Delicious heat filling her veins, she smiled up at him. *This is just the beginning of something very special.*

Several weeks later

She finished the last sweep of the cryogen wand over the now easily breathing patient. The patients were demonstrating tremendous strides and were transferring to medical floors.

The temperature was dropping to near normal and there was a hint of welcome moisture in the air. Levels of pollution and carbon dioxide were the lowest recorded in decades. A defense grid was deployed miles above Earth so that this horror could not be perpetuated on their unknowing vulnerable planet ever again.

The Luperan willingness to share their tech had turned the tide. The Luperans worked willingly and tirelessly alongside human counterparts. The cryogen tech was incredible. Kairn and his team were working with Earth's tech specialists to mass produce the units using reverse engineering and 3-D printers.

With Daria, Kairn was very approachable. He made himself available to her. He had spent so much time with Daria after her shifts that even Molly— as protective as she was—now looked forward to his visits. Daria smiled to herself and admitted freely that so did she. A lot. So...*Where is my Luperan? He is conspicuously absent.*

* * *

Finally back in the peaceful silence of his quarters, Kairn felt his ruff relax. It had taken a lunar cycle, punctuated with heated debate on many sides which nearly deteriorated into physical confrontations. Karin wished they had. Things would have gone more quickly without the political games-manship.

He sighed. The governments of Earth finally saw the criminal waste in dwelling on their superficial differences. Former enemies were becoming staunch allies in the battle to heal and protect their planet. It had been like herding feral Cascenti. Humans were proving stubborn, but fierce. He could see their potential.

The sun dipped beneath the horizon in a glorious blaze of golds, oranges, and pink. Staring at the stars blinking into sight in the darkening sky, he settled himself comfortably.

A subtle green scent teased his nose. His thoughts automatically turned to his Daria...his Mate. Behind him, another small bud unfurled into a tender blue leaf.

CHAPTER TEN

D aria woke to the rhythmic sound of his quiet breathing. She pillowed her head on his broad chest and heard his hearts beating for her. She rubbed her cheek against his light silky fur, the fine short hairs tickling her nose.

A growl rumbled in his chest and strong arms swept her over him. His breath was warm and sweet. Dipping his head, his lips followed the curve of her neck. His voice dropping another octave, he ground out. "Missed you so much, *Molindri*."

Her fingers threaded through his thick ruff as his lips touched hers softly in a teasing touch. His warm tongue brushed slowly again and again in a slow dance over her lips. His closed eyes slowly slitted open. His glowing eyes met hers. He took her lower lip and bit gently. She gasped as hunger flared hotly between them.

Daria panted and pulled him urgently against her. Hard muscles flexed and bunched as he settled hungrily into the cradle of her body. His large hands stroked gently down her spine. She heard a soft snick as he retracted his sharp claws. He traced his fingers over the points of her vertebrae—tickling her sensitive skin lightly in a delicious tease.

They shared a slow heated smile. His eyes closed. His velvety tail wrapped languidly around her ankle. With a soft groan, he urged her legs further apart. Her hips arched in urgent demand. His deep voice whispered her name reverently. "Daria...my Daria."

With a soft whimper, she parted her lips. His breath bathed her lips as he sighed. His tongue slowly explored her mouth—twining with her tongue before thrusting deep with a groan.

His taste. She felt the familiar touch of his mind brush against hers in a tender caress. She screamed. Her body clenched in almost painful pleasure—her vision going white.

Daria woke with a gasp, searching for his warmth. Her body was racked with fine shivers. She could remember the welcome weight and heat of his muscled body moving over her. She felt her desire, warm and slick, sliding slowly down her thighs. She throbbed and ached deep inside.

She still felt echoes of his devotion washing through her. Her thoughts tumbled over each other as she pored over the dream. *My imagination isn't that good...How could THAT be only a dream? It felt like a memory...like Déjà vu...*

Meanwhile...

Molindri!

Kairn came awake with a roar to images...no...memories of their mouths hotly, intimately mating. He was imprinting on her unique scent. His cock was engorged and painful. He could still taste echoes of her flavor on his tongue. The image of her curled trustingly on him seared irrevocably into his mind. Kairn smiled slowly. *I. Am. Hers.*

Meeting his Mate had triggered their Bond. His visions were strengthening, the exquisite details of this one burning in his mind. *I...we are bonding.*

Escalating waves of need and tenderness surged, heating his blood. Kairn smiled, even as he stalked into the privy, activated the cleanser, and adjusted the settings to cold.

CHAPTER ELEVEN

Daria found her attention wandering as the daily update wound down.

The hospital pace was back to its normal level of crazy. Her mind flashed to tantalizing half-remembered images in her dream. Of his jaw tracing along the sensitive juncture between her shoulder and neck. She licked her lips and thought she even caught a hint of his taste.

Heat flickered deep in her core. *If I'm very lucky, maybe I will dream of Kairn again tonight.*

With spiking consternation, Daria's head shot up. *What am I doing? I won't be able to look Kairn in the eye later today...not without turning bright red. He'll know something's different...*

Emily hip-bumped her affectionately. They were the last ones leaving the room, not wanting to bother with the bottleneck at the door. Emily lowered her voice. "So...were you day-dreaming about somebody special? You've got that Mona Lisa smile..."

Daria laughed softly. "You've been out the last week or so."

Daria paused with a blush. "Maybe..."

Shaking her head, Emily laughed. "Uh uh. You don't get away that easy. Don't leave me hanging. Catch me up, girlfriend."

Daria shook her head and kept walking. Emily stopped suddenly. Daria looked back at her in surprise. "What's..."

Emily shook her head. Everyone else had already left. Her voice echoed in the empty room. Her voice was uncharacteristically hesitant.

Her words rushed out in a flurry. "It's that Luperan ambassador, isn't it? You need to be careful. You may not know it, but he watches you all the time. Don't you find him intimidating? He looks like he's a CGI character out of one of those superhero movies we like."

Daria stared at Emily with rising worry. "You're serious, aren't you? Honey, he'd never hurt me. Kairn's been nothing but sweet with me. I thought you liked him."

Daria saw Emily shiver and wrap her arms around herself. "I like him fine...from a distance. He's been nothing but kind...But Daria, he has those claws and teeth."

Daria said slowly. "I don't even notice his teeth or claws anymore. He's just Kairn."

Daria's voice softened unknowingly. "My Kairn..."

Emily's face crumpled. Her eyes were wide with remembered horror at something only she could see. "It's too late. You already like him... way more than just like. I hope you're right...for your sake."

Emily seemed to shrink before her eyes. "Even a human man can do a lot of damage. These aliens...They're all so big...you couldn't stop them if they really wanted to hurt you!"

Daria paused, picking her words carefully. "Emily...did someone hurt you? A Luperan? I can tell Kairn. He'll punish them and make sure they never hurt you or anyone else again!"

Emily stared at her, her eyes nearly all black from her dilated pupils. Her voice was hoarse with strain. "It wasn't a Luperan. I'm sorry. I shouldn't have said anything."

Moving with deliberate care, Daria folded Emily's stiff body into a slow gentle hug. "We've been friends for years. You can tell me anything. Do you want to talk about it?"

Emily shook her head, the tension slowly draining from her. "No... Talking doesn't do me any good. I've seen enough counselors to know that much. It was a long time ago."

Emily pulled gently out of the hug. She met Daria's eyes squarely.

"Truly, it wasn't one of the Luperans. I can tell they're good people. They've always treated me with respect. I just sometimes panic. Flashback...I don't know."

Daria spoke quietly. "I'm going up to the cabin. Do you want to come with me? Just get away from everything for a while...we can talk... or not. Whatever you want. I don't want you to be by yourself right now."

Emily smiled sadly. "I'm fine, Daria. You're a good friend. I need to sort some things out. I need to be alone. I love you like a sister, but I need you to give me some space for a while. I won't do anything... impulsive. I'll call you as soon as I can."

Daria nodded slowly. "You'll call me if you need anything? Check in with me—at least by text. If something changes..."

Emily nodded, her usual humor trying to resurrect itself. "I know it. You'd drive like a bat out of hell to be there. Typically, with three state troopers in tow on your ass trying to keep up with you."

Taking the hint, Daria followed Emily's blatant cue to lighten the dark mood. "It was just the one time."

Emily's lips curled up in fond memory. "That you got caught. This isn't the Autobahn. There is the minor detail of a speed limit."

Daria grinned. "I don't remember the details. I'm pleading the 5th."

Emily fired back. "Likely story, little Miss Photographic Memory. I have a copy of the report. You showed it to me. They sounded impressed. The speed on those curves..."

Emily whistled softly. "Lights and sirens, girl. That kinda says it all."

Daria's grin faded. "Emily...if..."

Emily smiled. "I'll be alright. And I will call you if I need you. I'll never forgive you if you try anything official. I'm not suicidal by any stretch of your over-active imagination."

Emily stared meaningfully at Daria. Her eyes narrowing, Daria stared back at Emily. Daria began to absently twist a lock of hair around her finger in contemplation.

Emily smiled calmly. "I recognize your tells. Stop winding up your brain. I can hear your gears turning. You know me. I know when to call."

Daria relented with a reluctant sigh. "I trust you. Please don't prove me wrong on this."

Emily nodded solemnly. "I got this."

With her old insouciance, Emily flashed a wicked grin. "Besides, I know you. I'll live vicariously through you. Someone has to push you off the straight and narrow with your alien. That's my job!"

Emily hugged Daria. "Enjoy your time at the cabin. I will see you in a few."

Emily turned and walked briskly through the door.

Daria stared after her old friend, concern still jangling her nerves. She did know Emily all too well. *If I push too hard, Emily would just disappear for a few days completely incommunicado. Then where would we be?*

CHAPTER TWELVE

Daria

Still deep in thought, Daria walked the hall leading to her office. She came to a sudden happy stop as Molly weaved and bounced around her legs. "How'd you get out girl?"

A soft deep chuckle tickled her ears. "I was making the acquaintance of your canine again. Molly enjoys a good pet and having her ears scratched. As do I."

Daria smiled as a shiver of pleasure ran through her. She knew the rich bass tones before Kairn walked softly around the corner. Pleasure...and anticipation shivered through her...

Daria looked at his strong features and nearly lost herself in his amber eyes. She felt her pulse leap. He remembered Molly's name. She cleared her throat.

"We call her a dog."

She paused. "Am I repeating myself? I think I've told you that before, haven't I?"

Daria shook her head ruefully. Kairn took a careful step closer. His smile vanished as his gaze sharpened. Daria stifled the urge to lean even closer as his gaze lingered. A slow smile showed the sharp points of his canines. He gestured as his long sinuous tail started to swing gently. His smile widened. "My ancestors shared some traits with your dog. "

Daria knew her smile was strained. Her brain was still chasing down ways she could help Emily.

She tried to concentrate. Her words rushed out without a filter. "You're nothing like a dog! Oh God. You're so..."

Her cheek heating, Daria trailed off. "This is so awkward."

Daria's attention was being pulled in two very disparate directions. *What should I do about Emily? Should I call psych? She'd never forgive me... or trust me again.*

Her thoughts raced around like a rabbit hopped up on sugar. *And Kairn...I think he's maybe flirting. Surely not.*

Daria scolded herself. *I know better. I must be imagining things...because I want them...him so much.*

Daria grimaced. *I like myself, but I know good and well that I place education and work first. I'm damn good at my job. I'm always everyone's friend but have never had a...*

With a start, Daria remembered. Her thoughts jumped from one thing to another like a squirrel in a treasure trove of nuts. *Emily...How could I have forgotten?*

Her thoughts scattered. She could feel the warmth of his large body as he leaned forward, cupping his massive hand along her jawline. The callouses on his palm tickled gently. With a tender smile, he said, "*Molindri.* You should see your face. If only you knew just what I think of you. You're dedicated. Tireless. Kind. Fierce when you need to be. "

He eased his claws slowly through her hair, learning the texture and her unique scent. His voice was gently coaxing. "You are tired and need to rest. Come away with me. Let us learn from each other."

His voice dropped a register. "Apart from the obvious, we Luperans..."

Kairn paused, his eyes lingering on her face. "I am like your dog in some ways. We claim and protect what is ours. We defend with tooth and fangs. We are steadfast and loyal. We crave affection. Unlike them, when we choose our one—our Mate—we Bond for life."

Kairn leaned closer. His eyes were intent. "It is readily evident that something important is troubling you deeply. Put your brilliant mind at ease. Your problem is also mine. What can I...can we do to correct it?"

CHAPTER THIRTEEN

Kairn

Kairn listened intently as Daria related what little she knew of Emily's story. He felt mounting rage that anyone could injure a female in such an egregious fashion. That she still suffered the psychological effects was intolerable. He was silent as he thought furiously. *It is not possible for the male to be one of my people.*

His voice was even. "*Molindri*, it is not in our genetic composition to be capable of harming a female. Our instinct always seeks to protect. I will have my security officers investigate to be certain. They are meticulously thorough and will identify the cowardly perpetrator. Your friend will have her justice."

Kairn watched overt relief flicker across Daria's strained features upon sharing the sad burden of Emily's secret with him. He felt her relax and lean into his soothing touch.

Kairn spoke his thoughts aloud. "I will have a security detail monitor your friend at all times. They are very good at being undetected. She will not know they are there, but she will come to no harm. My word to you."

Daria breathed out a long sigh. "Thank you for doing this. Emily would have reacted...poorly if I had gone through standard human channels. It truly means a lot to me."

Kairn shook his head sharply. "No thanks are necessary. I feel an echo of your emotions. Your pain is mine. A burden shared is a burden

49

halved. As soon as I know, I will let you know what Lirinx—my head of security—discovers."

Daria smiled, relief and hope easily read in her eyes. Kairn stared at her and spoke his truth. "My hearts are gladdened that you entrust me with this. I hope you feel at ease with me. Please do not suppress the depth of your emotions. I want to be your rock...your safe place... always."

Kairn paused when he felt her arms slowly slide around his waist. He felt his hearts surge. "Each time you share them, we learn more of each other. Tell me your problems. We are stronger together. This builds trust between us."

He frowned darkly. "The words do not fit what I want to say."

Daria looked steadily at him and her pupils dilated. She cleared her throat. And again. "I think your words are just right."

Endearing color rose in her cheeks. Daria lifted her jaw with sweet fierceness. "So...I'm not sure. Is this a date?"

Kairn thought for a while. His brows shot northward. *Surely not.*

He frowned slightly. "A time heading?"

She shook her head. "People who are interested in each other spend time together to see if they develop deeper feelings. It's not as emotionally barren and mechanical as I make it out to sound."

Kairn took both her hands in his. Lowering his head, he nuzzled her back gently. He inhaled, her soft scent filling his lungs. He smiled ruefully. "Your language is an obstacle. I did not mean to hurt or confuse you."

His smile softened into pure sweetness. "Let me be clear. This is not a date."

Daria took a sharp breath and tried to wrest her hands loose from his. His smile widened. Kairn wrestled his hunger into submission. With careful control, he placed her hands over his hearts.

Kairn met her eyes. "This is our courtship. My hearts beat only for you. We will move at your pace but know that I am yours when you are ready."

Kairn forced himself to wait patiently. With a slow smile, he reminded himself. *Daria willingly shared her thoughts and concerns with me. She has asked for and accepted my help.*

His instincts were conflicted. They were clamoring madly for him to claim her now...and wanted to lavish her with tenderness. Kairn crushed them ruthlessly, reestablishing control over his surging emotions and instincts. *Daria...my Mate...has unknowingly branded me as hers.*

Kairn shook his head with a rueful grin. *But My Daria...my Mate... she does not realize the significance of what she has done.*

He counseled himself sternly. *Patience! Difficult though it is to accept, to my Daria, this is our beginning.*

CHAPTER FOURTEEN

Daria

After finishing a long shift, Daria suddenly remembered Emily comparing the Luperans to a tall drink of water. Daria mused. *On a very hot day.*

Daria frowned, worrying about her MIA friend. When last she saw him, Kairn had shared that Emily was safely tucked away in her cozy house and oblivious of her protective shadows.

Daria sighed deeply. *Emily has a point, but I couldn't disagree more. To me, Kairn is more like a big mug of hot chocolate made from scratch on a cold winter's night.*

She smiled to herself, absently tracing her lips. *Decadently satisfying with subtle layers of flavor. At the same time, somehow cozy and comforting. What a lovely, unexpected, and addicting combination.*

Daria's smile turned mischievous. *What would he say if he could hear my whimsical thoughts?*

A sudden thought crossed her mind. *What does he really taste like?*

She felt a blush heating her cheeks. The question lingered tantalizingly in her suddenly fevered brain.

Her pace slowed on the empty hallway to her office. Now she really wasn't looking forward to the drive home. The pace in the ICU was back to normal—even better with the drastic new treatments introduced by Luperan tech.

Along with a good number of her overworked staff, she had the next week off for some much needed relaxation. Daria tried to drum up some enthusiasm for it.

She loved her little cabin, but even with Molly's exuberant companionship, she felt a sharp pang of loneliness at the thought of going home to that empty house. Daria admitted to herself, *And I'll miss Kairn. I've gotten used to seeing him every day. I guess I'm a little spoiled...*

Daria thought back to how Kairn had asked for their "date," just as she had countless times since the moment he said it. She replayed his words in her head obsessively, turning them over and worrying about them like Molly with a bone—from every possible angle.

Daria sighed wistfully. *Courtship must have a different connotation for him than it does in English. Translators...I guess even intergalactic ones are glitchy. Stop pining, girl. You may as well wish for the moon.*

Despite her repeated admonishments to her lonely heart, Daria couldn't help the involuntary leap of her pulse when she found Kairn waiting patiently outside her office. He made it a point to walk her to her car at the end of her day whenever his schedule permitted. She paused a moment. *His schedule, hectic as it must be, somehow manages to allow for it a lot...not that I'm complaining! I like our...dates.*

Daria looked at him, soaking him in. *I feel like he's the one thing that I've been missing from my life for so long. I don't want to NOT be with him on my vacation. He means far too much to me already. I wonder...*

She felt suddenly shy. "I'm off duty for several days. Would you care to see some of the prettiest land I know up close?"

Kairn leaned over her and nuzzled her hair slowly. She heard him take a few slow deep breaths. Kairn smiled tenderly. "Is that your home?"

Daria colored slightly and nodded a slow yes.

Kairn bowed slightly and crooked an elbow for her. "I am honored that you would share this with me."

They let Molly out of her office and walked to the parking lot. They stared in silence at her large SUV. It was comfortably roomy for her and Molly, but one sheepish look showed that Kairn would never fit in her vehicle.

Daria looked askance at Kairn, who stared back with tender amusement. "I really want to show you where I live but..."

Kairn's eyes brightened to a soft gold. "That does pose a logistical problem."

Kairn inclined his head and nodded at the roof. "Why do we not take my vehicle? You can help me navigate."

Taking their time, they climbed up multiple flights. Daria basked in the simple pleasure of his undemanding company. Her eyes widened as they reached the rooftop. Daria walked around the shuttle in appreciation. Her eyes slid over the sleek aerodynamic angles greedily. Daria freely admitted that she had a lead foot. This ship was a beautiful machine, and she looked tantalizingly fast. *This craft has ruined cars for me.*

Daria trailed an idle hand along the sharply angled side. She gradually noticed the easy silence. Tearing her eyes away with difficulty, Daria looked up to find Kairn was watching her with a gentle smile. She smiled back with an unapologetic shrug. "I like fast cars...vehicles."

Kairn nodded with amused agreement. "There is something quite addictive about a fast vehicle. Especially if you have mountainous terrain."

Kairn adjusted the comm on his wrist. An opening appeared in the hull of the shuttle.

Molly jumped up from where she had been patiently sitting, barking eagerly.

Daria laughed. "Molly loves to ride. She loves to hang her head out of the window when I drive."

Kairn smiled. "This ship is set to manual control. It gives us a better feel for the terrain. Shall we see what she can do?"

Daria climbed in, following Molly's wildly wagging tail. "Ever notice that ships are addressed as female? We do that here on Earth as well."

Kairn sealed the door behind him. He had a whimsical smile on his face. "That is true. I had never paid much attention before, but we address the Guardian as our lady."

He shook his head at the memory. "I cannot keep track of the many times I have had Breis, our head engineer, tell me, 'She has given us all she can.' My answer is generally, 'Ask her again. She will give us more. She always does. Our lady takes care of us.'"

Kairn nodded slowly. "I think it is a sign of affection and respect. If we take care of her, she takes care of us."

They shared a look of tender amusement layered with deepening understanding.

CHAPTER FIFTEEN

Kairn

Daria's head turned from side to side. Seeing the familiar through her eyes, Kairn smiled slowly. *The view from the shuttle was truly breathtaking.*

The Water levels were gradually rising. The wind raced over the wide expanse of blue ocean, leaving frothy white caplets in its wake. With barely contained awe, Daria stared wide eyed around the cabin. Her voice had an endearing squeak. "You can see so clearly. I can't believe...Holy Gene Roddenberry, I'm in a spaceship!"

Kairn watched her with an indulgent smile. He absently responded. "The armor is transparent over the bridge."

He paused, mentally reviewing the topography. "Do you want to pilot her? It is an easy, short flight..."

Kairn caught himself, but Daria hadn't noticed his slip. Her voice was breathy with excitement. "If you...What if I..."

Kairn laughed softly, "I will be right here. It is not unlike driving one of your cars...Just much faster."

Daria shot him an incredulous look. Her fingers twitched. His voice was calm and gently amused. "Stay on this heading. We are following the edge of the coast. We will keep her over the water for now."

He touched the instrument board and switched control to the copilot. He leaned back in his chair.

Fascinated, he watched her features light up as she studied the controls.

Daria had narrowed her eyes in fierce concentration. He nodded slightly in approval. *She has a good, light touch on the controls. She looks to be a natural.*

A sensor beeped. He arched a brow in interest. His voice was light. "You are doing very well. Maintain your speed and angle the directional control until it reads 45 degrees. Program elevation to 75 feet over the Water."

They flew over the vast deep blue of the Pacific Ocean. The smooth expanse was broken only by the crests of small waves. His voice was calm and proud. "You have done a phenomenal job. You will be an amazing pilot."

Kairn saw Daria flash him a look of joyous disbelief. He said calmly, "We should be coming up on them now."

Daria flicked him a questioning glance. She echoed softly. "Them?"

The shuttle wobbled slightly before Daria steadied her hands. She stared raptly out the viewing screen. Sleek dark grey bodies leaped out of the water. Daria's voice was quiet with wonder. "Dolphins...a pod of dolphins..."

Kairn flicked a control. "Magnify and amplify audio and visual input. Engage autopilot. Match speed."

A raucous symphony of clicks and squeaks filled the cabin. Kairn saw her eyes begin to water. She sniffed. He reached quickly for her. Smiling brightly, Daria's voice was shaky. "Happy...tears."

She met him halfway and snuggled close over his left chest. They could see intelligent dark eyes studying them each time a dolphin leapt out of the water. The pod had stopped to study their shuttle and was swimming in wide circles. Kairn adjusted the instruments. "Connect to comms. Hover and lower to elevation 40 feet."

Kairn opened the shuttle door. Together, Daria and Kairn leaned out and stared at the dolphins, one of whom pointedly stared back - openly curious.

Kairn said softly, "We mean you no harm. You are magnificent. We wanted to say hello."

Excited squeaks and clicks answered him. Kairn smiled. "She thanks us. Her name is Dives Deep. She is the pod leader. She says the water is much cleaner and sweeter. She says welcome to their world... and invites us to play."

Daria looked at him hopefully. Kairn shook his head with sincere regret. "We do not have the appropriate gear today."

He thought for a moment. "But we have enough fuel to enjoy a good visit."

He paused at the cascade of whistles and squeaks. "And a standing invitation to come back."

Daria reached her arms around him as far as she could. She hugged him tight and dropped a jubilant kiss over his hearts. "I can't...I want... Thank you for sharing this with me. I'm so glad we did this together. This has been the best day."

After they spent a pleasant hour or two visiting with Dives Deep and her family, Daria piloted the shuttle back to the coast. Kairn smiled proudly at her calm competence. He took the helm before they made the turn over the jagged treetops. *That would be a piloting lesson for another day.*

They followed the winding coastline until they landed near her home. Daria had noted only absently that Kairn did not need much help at all with directions.

Kairn noted the fine details. Her small cottage was nestled against the dense surrounding tree line with a wide grassy meadow leading to the cliff side. Wildflowers added bright dots of color to the lush green of the grass. Clear sunshine washed the land in gentle golden light. The ocean tasted alive. He savored the vibrant bite of salt on his tongue.

Kairn felt a burgeoning sense of relief and welcome. He soaked in the many details he...remembered. His lips curved in a brilliant, sweet smile. He tucked Daria, trusting and soft, into his side.

Kairn pulled his boots off and ran his feet through the thick cushiony grass. His sensitive nose parsed out each distinctive detail. This world had such a bounty of natural gifts. Molly belatedly woke up from a nap. The dog dashed madly ahead of them up the path and pushed through the dog door. Kairn and Daria walked slowly up the worn path.

He lingered at the short bushes lushly lining the long walkway, his attention caught by the tall, spiky bluish flowers and silvery green foliage. He sniffed appreciatively at the complex fragrance...sweet with a pleasantly sharp herbal finish. It was the same note that lingered on Daria, layering over her own unique scent.

His attention snapped to Daria when she murmured his name. She gestured toward the plants, her voice was rich with gentle amusement. "I like the lavender too."

Daria paused, her hand resting on the door. She warned him, "It's comfortable, but it's nothing fancy."

His voice deepened. Kairn leaned closer as his eyes flared. "I have liked...much more than merely liked everything I have seen."

Daria met his eyes, her cheeks flushing a pretty pink. She unlocked the heavy door. He looked at her, arching a brow. He opened it. Kairn sniffed the air carefully. "If you permit me, I would like to secure the premises."

Daria nodded slowly. "I'd like that. If we've been out, I usually let Molly check it out before I go in."

Kairn smiled, relaxing a bit. "Good idea. I do not smell anything worrisome, but I would like to do a visual check."

Kairn grinned at her. He did a quick, detailed walkthrough. He nodded to himself in satisfaction.

The structure was well-built and would hold up to severe weather well. The house was secure. There had been no unwelcome visitors in his Mate's absence.

Kairn met her back at the front door with a reassuring smile and followed her in. He heard her secure the dog door. Kairn stood in the middle of the room with an air of appreciation.

The room was large with (thankfully) high ceilings. His nose was tickled by the dry scent of wood and the smoky echo from an old fire in the large fireplace. Worn smooth, the floorboards shone with the soft patina of age. The room was cool and flooded with natural light from the large windows.

Against a central large window, a sturdy sofa with deep cushions beckoned invitingly. Scattered woven rugs and pillows added bright touches. Jewel toned glass sculptures sat on wide windowsills, glowing in the sunshine and refracting a rainbow of color into the room. Daria opened the windows to air out the room. A gentle breeze brought in the fragrance of sun-warmed grass spiced with the pleasant bite of lavender and the haunting call of birds on the wing.

CHAPTER SIXTEEN

Daria

Daria sat on the sofa, curling comfortably into a deep corner. She'd thrown the makings for beef stew in the slow cooker. Delicious aromas reminiscent of rich tomatoes, earthy root vegetables, savory spices, and hearty beef wafted from the kitchen, making her mouth water.

Daria smiled as she saw Kairn take a long, appreciative sniff. She could feel him relaxing even more. With a quizzical smile, she watched Kairn explore the room. The long tufts of his large ears were a comfortable three or so feet from the exposed rafters of her twelve-foot ceiling. His height and heavily muscled build made the large room and her oversized furniture feel deliciously intimate.

Light glinted subtly off glass. Kairn looked quizzically at Daria who smilingly nodded. He carefully picked up a sculpture in his fingers, claws retracting. It was one of a set of four. He had a strong sense of motion and leashed power. When together, they seemed to move...no, that was not the word...they swam, seeming to ripple smoothly through the surface of the dark wood.

Daria said softly, "That's the Loch Ness Monster. He's part of Earth's folklore, rumored to still live in a deep lake."

Kairn set it back in place with care, his long fingers running along the smooth glass in appreciation. Daria watched the smooth sure glide of his fingers and felt heat bloom in her body. Her nipples tingled and an ache built slowly in her core.

He moved on to the next piece. Suspended from the ceiling with barely visible metallic wire, the sleek lines embodied grace and freedom. With marked delicacy, Kairn traced a sharp claw along the finely etched wing of the rearing horse who seemed to spin and dance with the eddying movements of the air.

Daria felt her skin flush and felt rich hot moisture build between her legs. Her nipples were hard and tender, abraded by the soft cotton of her T-shirt. She cleared her throat, "Pegasus, a winged horse ridden by mythical gods of old Earth."

Daria pulled her knees up on the sofa to hide her nipples. Kairn looked at her with a slight smile, but his eyes were alight with stark turbulent hunger. He moved to the next sculpture, splintering prisms of light in the sunlight.

His eyes lit with fond memories on the next piece—a remarkably life-like dolphin rendered in shimmering grey glass. Kairn looked up and met her eyes with a sweet smile, stroking his fingers along the smooth sides.

Kairn next picked up a beautifully detailed dragon with an appreciative growl. There was a lot of crystal he had yet to explore. Daria swallowed hard. *This is sheer torture. Delicious tantalizing foreplay drawn out for what feels like forever!*

Her fingers itched to touch the thin layer of silky fur overlying his hard muscles. She stared at the sleek muscles of his broad shoulders as they curved into the powerful lines of his back. Daria resisted the urge to fan her heated face. *Dear Lord, he had a truly spectacular back.*

Kairn turned, slowly cradling a crystal ballerina in his hands. With an appreciative smile, he ran a caressing finger along the ballerina's gracefully arched spine. Daria could barely hear over her pulse roaring in her ears. She stared at Kairn's eyes...his usually amber pupils were now shot through with burning molten gold.

CHAPTER SEVENTEEN

Kairn

Kairn placed the ballerina gently back in her spot. The intoxicating subtle notes of Daria's arousal perfumed the air, a rich musky fragrance he could almost taste. It spurred vibrant memories of his vision. His dream. He was trying to give her time to accept him, but his control unraveled.

He reached out with a guttural growl as she leaned forward eagerly. He swept her into his arms and held her close against his chest. With wonder, he took note of how her head fit so neatly against his hearts. He could not remember when he'd taken off his shirt. His hearts stuttered, then raced even faster as she nuzzled into his soft fur.

When Daria reached up for him, Kairn lifted her body so that her head was level with his. He stared into her hunger-glazed eyes. She smiled and set about learning the brutally elegant lines of his face with slow, aching deliberation. With a sigh of sublime appreciation, she buried her hands deep in his ruff.

Her scent was wonderfully, dearly familiar. Daria traced his soft lips. Kairn's breath hitched. She laughed softly as he dropped butterfly kisses on her fingers. He nibbled softly on her exploring fingertips. She groaned when his tongue teased between her fingers. He growled as he reveled in his first taste of her skin.

Kairn pulled her hand in closer. He drew her finger into his mouth and sucked softly on it. Her taste sank home. His eyes slid shut as he sucked hard. Daria's body twisted wildly. "Kairn...I can't..."

Her voice trailed off. He nipped a little sharply. She screamed softly as her body arched into his hips with surprised pleasure—rubbing slowly, demandingly over his aching cock. His hips thrust in a slow teasing grind. She groaned out, "Don't...oh there...don't tease me."

Kairn slid her finger carefully out with a soft parting kiss. Their eyes met as he lowered his head and brushed his lips softly over hers. Slow fleeting touches of light pressure. Back and forth. He caught a quick glimpse of her pink tongue as she licked her lips. His tongue slowly chased the moisture along the seam of her lips.

She gasped, lips parting. Her flavor exploded on his tongue. Growling deep in his chest, he helplessly thrust slow and deep into her mouth in search of her elusive tongue. It slid slick...smooth...warm against his in welcome, slow teasing strokes as he explored her delicate depths.

Her hands ran slowly over his lightly furred chest. Daria slowly slid her body against his. He growled as the hard points of her nipples dragged through the fine thin layer of his fur...teasing his skin. Their kiss grew hungrier and deeper, their tongues mating.

Kairn retracted his claws and traced the length of her back. He gently massaged the taut muscles in slow circles along her spine. He mapped the sensitive point where the top of her thighs flowed into her hips.

He sent a careful finger along the top of the deep crease dividing her ass. Traced it down slowly. Warmth radiated invitingly as her legs moved restlessly further apart. With a deep growl of hunger, Kairn cursed the thin layers of material separating their skin.

CHAPTER EIGHTEEN

Kairn

Long moments…minutes spent immersed in shared pleasure. He lost any perception of time. A sudden noise drew his attention. Feeling nearly drunk with waves of tenderness spiced with a liberal dose of hunger, he lifted his head reluctantly. Their lips clung together as she nuzzled closer.

The light was now only gently washing the room. A loud bark. And again. Molly danced urgently at the door. Kairn threaded his fingers carefully through Daria's hair, stroking the tousled locks back behind her ears. He dropped a gentle kiss on her upturned nose, startling a delightful burble of laughter from her.

He inclined his head toward a loudly indignant Molly and winced. He shrugged into his uniform, leaving the fastener open. Daria caught his fingers as he turned toward the door. She said softly, "Rain check?"

Kairn opened the door. Molly bounded out. He sniffed deeply at the air. Studied the clear skies. He thought he could convince himself of a few non-threatening fluffy clouds in the distance. He turned a quizzical look toward Daria.

He saw her eyes study his face and linger on his now swollen lips. She laughed, mischief mixed with sweet warmth glinting in her eyes. He saw her face flush warmly as she continued, "Something postponed that I want. A lot."

Her eyes burned. "Again. Soon."

Kairn felt his canines lengthen. He took a step toward her. "Many rain checks."

Her eyes were soft with a hunger that mirrored his. A low growl rumbled continuously in his chest. He ground out. "Now."

She was moving to him when he heard a loud thud near his feet. Molly was poised eagerly at his side, a large paw resting hopefully on an extraordinarily large piece of wood. A hopeful woof was accompanied by soulfully imploring eyes.

Kairn groaned at the pitiful sight. A soft giggle shook Daria's shoulders as she snuggled close into his side. Resigned, he bent over to retrieve the good-sized log and heaved it off. As Molly took off in joyful search, he heard Daria mutter distinctly...mournfully. "Cockblocker."

Kairn looked down in alarm and felt melting relief at her broad grin. He hugged her closer. He felt a rueful grin tug at his lips. "That was self-explanatory. And sadly, quite literal in translation."

His voice rippled with amusement even as he grimaced slightly. He caught Daria's involuntary glance at the long length of his cock pushing against the reinforced placket of his uniform. Kairn shook his head at the burgeoning apology he saw in her eyes.

"Well worth it."

Still smiling, he touched his forehead gently to hers. Molly gamboled back up to them. They shared rueful laughter at the log balanced comically in Molly's jaws—with jagged ends projecting easily a foot out on either side. Kairn sighed as Molly neatly deposited the log into his dutifully waiting palm. Daria pressed closer and caught his lower lip in her teeth, nipping it gently. She said quietly, "Rain."

Kairn finished softly, his eyes half closing with pleasure, "Check."

CHAPTER NINETEEN

Daria

From her vantage point deep in the warm soft grass, Daria watched with an indulgent smile as Kairn played fetch with her dog. Molly was beside herself with glee, hunting down the branch (really, it was a log) as Kairn pitched it far across the meadows and into the tree line. Over and over again. Until Molly flopped down in happy exhaustion at her side, lapping at the water bowl Daria had ready.

Daria patted the spot to the right of her. Kairn gracefully settled himself in the grass. He took the large bottle of water she handed him with a warm smile of thanks, their fingers grazing and then lingering in a silent promise. With a low groan of contentment, Kairn leaned back on his elbows—utterly at ease and basking in the sunlight.

As he moved, his uniform pulled tight across his wide chest as his muscles bunched and shifted smoothly. Daria stared a moment—mourning the fact that he had absently shrugged into his jacket. Her fingers twitched. Daria absently registered his voice.

She forced herself to look up from his chest and found herself caught in his tenderly amused eyes. Daria cleared her throat and awkwardly began, "What did you say?"

She felt a blush rising and lifted a hand to her hot cheeks. She choked out, "I didn't m-mean to stare. I'm s-sorry..."

She faltered to a stop when he lifted a slow hand, his long fingers cool against her heated skin.

His voice was gentle, but his voice was rough with heat. "I hope we are beyond shallow social customs. I like that you are shy. I enjoy you. I want you to say what you think. I want you to be curious about me—as I am about you."

His voice deepened even more. "I am eternally glad you like looking at me. I want you to touch me."

His eyes were soft and hungry as he lay back in the grass. He casually folded his arms under his head.

Daria's eyes drifted along his sleek muscles of his biceps; they were sharply defined by his uniform's snug fit. He was a feast for her senses. She leaned closer. His spicy scent suddenly was richer and touched with masculine musk. He looked so tempting laying in the grass.

Daria slowly lay down next to him. She could feel the warmth of his body. With a shy heated look, Daria murmured, "I don't know where to start."

His voice velvety soft, Kairn smiled at her. "Wherever you like, *Molindri.*"

She relaxed as they stared at each other. Karin lay very still, though she could see the controlled tension in his muscles. His voice was soft. "I want...need you to be at ease with me."

Daria frowned. She searched for the right words. "I really enjoy you and..."

She remembered that kiss. He tasted rich, spicy, and wild. She fought to find the right words. "I have feelings for you I can't explain or name. I miss you when you're not with me. We enjoy each other. I think I'm falling in love with you, but it's happening so fast."

She took a deep breath and gestured down the length of their bodies. She said in a rush, "I've never done this before."

Kairn's gaze was steady as he stared back at her. He said calmly, "Uncivilized though it may make me seem, it gladdens my hearts to share this with you."

His cheeks flared with a soft, rich blue. He smiled slightly. "I have never done this either. It is only right that we learn this together."

Daria stared at him in delighted wonder. She realized she felt a bone-deep satisfaction that he had not ever shared his body with anyone else. He smiled knowingly, hunger burning deep in his eyes. His tone was matter of fact. He stated simply...proudly, "I am yours. I was waiting for you."

His words seemed to repeat on an endless loop in her ears. Daria shifted absently, trying to find a good spot for her head. Kairn lifted an elbow in silent invitation. She hesitated, her eyes lingering on the hard curves. She shook her head slowly. "No."

She saw a flash of hurt in his eyes, quickly camouflaged. Daria rolled over and gently lay her head on his left chest. She tilted her head and read the open relief written on his face. He was so starkly honest. He was committed to this.

Daria fingered the jacket fastenings he had only partially done up. "May I?"

Daria could feel his breath catch. Kairn groaned with a singularly sweet smile. "Please..."

Daria rested her trembling hands on the placket of his uniform. The soft snick of the fastenings slowly coming undone sounded unusually loud. With a soft sigh, Daria rubbed her cheek and jaw over the thin layer of his soft plush fur. She nuzzled closer until she heard the steady thrum of his hearts in her ear.

She listened to his quiet breathing. She heard it catch for long moments as she stroked his chest with curious gentle fingers—exploring... learning his broad heavy sweep of muscles. Her voice was shy as she felt them begin to tremble under her learning touch. Daria lifted her hand slowly, regretfully. "I'm not trying to tease you."

He brought his left arm down and cuddled her closer. With a soft growl, he caught her fingers. Squeezing them gently, he replaced them in that same spot on his chest. Kairn moved her hand slowly under his, felt her hand resume its tantalizing movement.

He smiled gently; embers of hunger banked in his soft eyes. "You are not teasing me. Please do not stop. I am a patient hunter. You are well worth the wait."

His eyes closed briefly as he sought control. He smiled with singular sweetness, spiced with ever present hunger. His voice vibrated with the depth of his emotions. "I am savoring your every touch. Please touch me. Your pleasure is also mine. We do this at your pace."

Daria stared at him and slowly petted him, marveling at his sleek, soft fur. She felt a hard jolt of pleasure run through him. She ran her hand down the fine, short fur, accidentally ruffling it against the grain on the backstroke. His muscles twitched uncontrollably under her hand and helpless laughter rippled from his thrown-back head. Tenderness rushing through her, Daria stared at him in fascinated bemusement. *Well...hell. A secret weapon!*

Eyes dancing with mischief, her hands ruffled his fur with ruthless glee. Carefree minutes flew by as she laughingly launched a double-handed frontal assault. Kairn ever-so-carefully tried to defend his sorely besieged self...only to be unsuccessful in a truly merciless rout of his defenses.

He panted, a wide, delighted grin on his face as she collapsed on his heaving chest with a snort laugh. Daria gasped out, "Victorious!"

Kairn managed to pant out, "Unconditional...surrender."

Daria felt the deeper meaning weaving through his words. She stared at him. His breath settled. Slowly, his grin softened into *her* smile. For the first time, she noticed that he never smiled like that for anyone else.

Daria paused, then leaned forward and dropped a light kiss over his hearts. That smile...it grew bigger, wilder, and sweeter—even as his eyes watched her with patient understanding and banked hunger.

She touched his chest and left her hand squarely over his strong hearts. "Thank you. For playing with me."

She felt his hearts thud harder under her fingers. She could feel his voice vibrate in his deep chest. "For your trust. Always. My pleasure."

CHAPTER TWENTY

Kairn

They rested, curling together on the bed of soft, fragrant grass. Kairn took a long, thoughtful look at them. Daria's clothes were liberally decorated with grass stains. Somehow he had lost his uniform shirt.

He was sweating lightly from the exertion with broken blades of grass sticking to his fur. Kairn was fairly certain he had twigs and bits of grass tangled in his tousled hair.

Daria's hair was mussed in what she had offhandedly declared "bed head." She looked enchanting.

He thought for a moment. That bit of slang did not require explanation. Kairn hoped he would one day see Daria's legitimately earned "bed head."

He noticed all this as Daria continued to pet him gently, unconsciously possessive, over his hopeful hearts. Kairn breathed a deep sigh of contentment. He memorized everything in its minutest detail. This moment was one he would treasure for every day of his long lifetime.

He heard Daria laugh suddenly. She slanted an incredulous look at him, her shoulders shaking with mirth. "Ticklish...Really?!"

Kairn hid his smile and intoned officiously. "I am a great Luperan warrior. I have no weaknesses. I do not acknowledge this puny tickling. I will de..."

His mask fractured in a torrent of laughter as Daria darted her hand in a quick riff over his hard, ridged belly.

Daria paused, her fingers poised in prime tickling position. She dug her index finger into his lightly furred muscle and started a small ruffle. His muscle jumped under her touch. She smiled, "One last chance. Surrender now or suffer my wrath!"

Kairn eyed the gently wriggling finger with no little wariness. "I yield. Parlay!"

She tilted her head in consideration. Mischief blended with heat in an intoxicating combination. Daria smiled, "To the victor belong the spoils. Surrender demands a forfeit."

Kairn fervently conceded, "Anything."

He elaborated slowly. "Name your terms."

Her eyes suddenly were serious. "We have so much fun together."

Playfully, she then seamlessly fell back into her role. "Let me think on it."

Her smile was suddenly wicked and intimate. She dropped a soft kiss on his lips, licked the seam of his lips. "Rain check."

He laughed, his eyes gleaming with promises.

* * *

Kairn kept a protective arm around Daria. She was still asleep. She had slid off his chest and had burrowed into his side. She grumbled sleepily and moved, settling back down with her head over his hearts.

Kairn smiled tenderly as he watched her. He made a conscious effort and checked his comms every few hours, getting updates from Darzik. Nothing yet on Emily.

On a more positive note, the stabilization of the planet was going well and nearly on schedule. He looked at Daria and caught himself. *The planet's...My Daria's planet is named Earth.*

As he perused the latest reports, Kairn paused. From his tone, Darzik was quite impressed—a difficult feat for anyone to achieve. Breis, his lead engineer in the Guardian and an old friend, had been very busy.

He was a mechanical wizard who took the current status of Earth's so-called green energy programs as a personal affront.

Breis had gutted, tweaked, and rebuilt entire systems. In the process, he had managed to upgrade the efficacy of Earth's solar and wind harvesting systems more than a thousand percent and designed a CO_2 eliminator which produced Water as a byproduct in his spare time.

Kairn felt teeth showing in a grin. Kairn was proud of his crew. Unerringly, they managed to rise to all occasions with commendable grace. They managed to exceed even his admittedly lofty expectations and reset the bar for those to follow.

Their human counterparts were motivated and quick learners. Darzik had made specific notes where they had suggested promising innovative ideas. Kairn sighed. *I need to be back at the command base in the morning.*

Kairn looked at Daria sleeping peacefully in the setting sun. She needed to rest after the long shifts she put in. He constantly heard good things about her from his human liaisons. He reluctantly slid her head gently onto the grass. Looking around, he salvaged his shirt.

Kairn turned it so that only the soft side faced out—tucking it under her head. He stood with growing reluctance. Kairn looked sharply over at Molly who had been dozing, sprawled in the grass. At Kairn's silent command, she trotted swiftly over, stationing herself alertly at Daria's side. Kairn scratched her ears briefly and then headed for his ship.

After several minutes, Kairn came back with a large bag. With gentle hands, he checked on a still napping Daria. He nodded briefly in approval to a watchful Molly. Kairn took another look at Daria and walked swiftly to the tree line. He was quickly lost in the growing shadow of the dense branches.

CHAPTER TWENTY-ONE

Daria

Daria stretched. The sun was a lot lower in the sky. She'd had a very good nap. She looked around for Kairn, but didn't see him. A comforting, familiar fragrance tickled her nose. Daria nuzzled closer and shifted her head on her soft pillow. She smiled in sudden anticipation. *Pillow?*

She sat up and looked behind her at the neatly folded uniform. She sniffed delicately at the material. She could still smell traces of his wild, spicy scent. She touched the bundle with a gentle finger. A wondering smile dawned on her face. *It was the little things...*

She sat in the warm grass, scratching behind Molly's ears lazily. Molly's large frame lay protectively in front of her. Though she flicked her large ears in answer, Molly kept her attention focused.

Daria's gaze wandered over the large meadow and surrounding forest. Sometimes, she took it for granted. She soaked it in. The horseshoe shape naturally framed the cliffs overlooking the ocean. The large meadow was bordered by old forest.

It was a lovely sight. It was remote and peaceful here. She had no close neighbors. She had a generator with solar back up. A deep well supplied ample sweet artesian water. Her cisterns preserved the generous rainwater. A water reclamation system repurposed bath and kitchen water into her garden. Her home was self-sufficient. The rest of the world seemed so far away. It was the perfect place to restore body and mind.

With a slow smile curving her lips, Daria was enjoying the acrobatic derring-do of the squirrels leapfrogging between the trees. Molly eased to her feet, her attention on the tree line. Daria saw Kairn emerge from the forest, crossing the wide meadow quickly.

Daria stared in surprise when Molly trotted to intercept him. Molly positioned herself in front of Kairn and let out a series of escalating yips and barks. Daria watched as Kairn spoke softly to her dog. Molly barked sharply and stalked back to Daria's side.

Daria watched Kairn quizzically. He had a look of quiet satisfaction as he walked over to them. He sank gracefully into the grass to her right. Daria leaned against his side, "What was that about? I've never seen her behave like that. I thought she liked you."

Kairn grinned. "She does. She just wanted to let me know that she would happily tear me apart if I hurt you. Molly loves you very much."

His grin mellowed into her smile. "I assured her that I would never hurt you if I could, at all, prevent it."

Daria melted into his side. Kairn lifted his arm, curling it around her protectively...instinctively. She nuzzled until she found her spot over his hearts. She arched a brow with a smile, "Did Molly really say that?"

Daria stiffened. She was quiet for a moment. "Your comm...Have you heard anything yet about Emily?"

Kairn slowly shook his head. "Nothing in Earth's data banks under her name going back more than five Earth years. They are still searching for any suspicious males or unsolved cases involving females of her age."

He stroked his jaw over her head absently. "Lirinx sends regular reports. She is safe. She is on recuperation time. Something he says is called vacation. She is making routine stops at a weapons training area. She is much more relaxed after these visits. Lirinx says she is admirably proficient with a primitive projective weapon. High praise from my weapons expert."

Kairn paused with a thoughtful smile. "My XO, Darzik, is an old and trusted friend...my brother. While being very mindful of her triggers, he is forming a deep attachment to Emily."

After a considering moment, Daria smiled slowly. "He may very well be exactly what she needs, but he will need to be very patient."

Kairn rubbed his jaw absently along her temple in an instinctive caress. "Darzik is one of the best males I know...and a patient hunter. She will have all the time she needs."

With a wistful smile, Daria looked up at Kairn. "I just really want her to be alright. I wish she'd let us help her."

Kairn tightened his arms around her. "*Molindri*, I know you do. You cannot force your friend to do anything. When she is ready, you...we will be there to help her. Until then, we will watch over her and ensure that she comes to no harm."

Daria frowned slightly. "There is an old adage that holds true. You can lead a horse to water, but you can't make her drink."

Kairn frowned slightly and then grinned slowly. "The herbivore is rumored to be quite independent. I understand the analogy. It is indeed an apt one."

Daria shook her head bemusedly. *He is right. These things can't be rushed. We will take one day at a time.*

A bright smile grew on her face. She deliberately changed the subject. "The computer on the shuttle. The translator...really? So...I'd forgotten. I had thought it was the shuttle's computer that allowed you to talk with them."

His jaw continued to rub lightly over her head without missing a beat. Kairn rumbled softly. "Mmmmm. Dives Deep was the work of the shuttle computer. Personal translators improve and learn with exposure to the language."

Daria felt him kiss the top of her head. Kairn rumbled in a quiet voice, "Molly said you found her on the side of the road headed out here. She remembers being alone, wet and cold. Scared and hungry."

He paused, "She emphasized the scared and hungry part a lot. Molly knows you are not her mother, but that is how she identifies you."

Kairn reached out to rub Molly gently over her ears. Daria ran her hand slowly along Molly's back and met Kairn's eyes. He anticipated Daria's inevitable question. "You cannot have one. There is no predictable safety profile in humans."

Kairn was adamant. "They have never been used by humans. They are neural implants. I have had one since I joined the Alliance service."

He felt Daria take a deep breath. His voice was unyielding as he repeated himself. "You cannot have one. Your neural pathways have not been adequately mapped."

Kairn's ears twitched in confusion when he heard Daria mutter darkly, "I am sorry. I do not think I heard you correctly. You are not a small furry rodent with a twitching nose...this guinea pig."

Daria sighed and elaborated. "Figure of speech."

Kairn's ears twitched again. "Slang..."

His eyes narrowed. Daria rubbed her neck and came up with a quick rough explanation. "Colloquial phrase in English language. Not meant to be taken laterally."

His eyes intent, Kairn nodded sharply. Daria couldn't help her wry tender smile. *He really was trying to understand.*

She went on, "I know that's the smart thing. But someone's going to have to be the first guinea pig."

Daria smiled knowingly. "It's you. You would monitor the smallest detail. I couldn't be in better hands. Why *not* me?"

Kairn stared for a long moment. When he finally spoke, his voice was a deep growl. "While I treasure the trust you put in me, I will never put you at unreasonable risk like that. Do not ever demand that of me. I will not...cannot relent on this point."

Daria nodded reluctantly. "I know. I don't mean to abuse your trust. I'm sorry for asking that. It's just that it would be so great to talk with her..."

Kairn's arm tightened and she nuzzled closer. They watched the slow path of the sinking sun across the clear sky. In the evening light, wild birds flew across the meadow on their way home.

Together, they watched the sun set beyond the horizon in a glorious light show. The sky exploded, bright gold shading into a rich kaleidoscope of oranges, pinks, and purples.

Without the sun, the temperature dropped considerably with a distinct nip in the air. With a hum of contentment, Daria leaned into his body heat. Kairn draped his shirt over her shoulders, grinning when the hem brushed her mid-calf. They headed toward the house in a companionable silence.

Kairn commented absently, "Even among Earth's admittedly eclectic dialects, English is an eccentric language."

He paused. "I thought you were American. Does your America not have a language of her own? Why do you speak English?"

With a rueful smile, Kairn waited patiently as she dissolved again into fits of giggling.

CHAPTER TWENTY-TWO

Kairn

Daria had made a meal of something she called beef stew. Thick savory sauce coated a wide variety of legumes. There were generous portions of large, tender chunks of meat spiced to a delicious blend of flavors. Thick, soft slices of delicately flavored, golden baked grain complimented the meat and sopped up the rich juices beautifully. The feast of scents made his nose twitch in delighted anticipation.

Daria had laughed softly as he eyed the vegetables dubiously and ate them last. He had not cared as much for the vegetables, but he suspected...hoped they were an acquired taste.

He reminded himself Daria had called the dense, white starchy ones potatoes. The orange, sweet ones were carrots. The green, ridged ones were celery.

Kairn assumed...hoped he was going to be the fortunate recipient of large quantities of these. More vegetables meant more meals and priceless time spent with his Mate.

Between them, they had managed to devour most of the large container. Kairn corrected himself. *I have had three large bowls to Daria's single small one.*

His belly was comfortably full. They had given the remaining drippings and small pieces of meat to an ecstatic Molly. In the next room, he could still hear Molly gnawing happily on the large soup bone.

Contentedly, Kairn watched Daria moving around her food preparation area. She had changed into comfortable stretchy pants.

She had appropriated his shirt and was still wearing it. Kairn relished the sight of her small body engulfed in something he had worn close to his body.

His attention sharpened. *Did she just take a sniff of my shirt?*

He watched as she closed her eyes, a sweet smile curving her lips. Karin felt the now familiar need hammer through his system. His hunger was tempered by an ever-deepening sweetness. He could feel their link...their priceless Bond growing.

Daria was learning to trust him. Her touches, tentative at first, were growing in confidence. He rubbed his chest right over his hearts. They raced, filling with aching tenderness. Kairn sent up a fervent prayer that the tantalizing eternity inherent in the poignant moment would never end.

He perused his memories, reflecting on them with tenderness and remembered pleasure. *It has been such an amazing day. Her bright mind. Her humor. Her affection. The loyalty she inspired in her canine companion. Her open response to me...the eager echoed hunger in her touch. Not even in my wildest imaginings did I ever dare to hope for this. We are finding such joy in each other.*

She was making one of her favorite treats to share with him. His nose twitched as an array of startling scents teased it. Daria carefully stirred the white liquid in the pan over the heating element. He reminded himself. *Milk.*

His nose twitched in mild apprehension. *It smells bland and not particularly appetizing. On the stove. My grasp of English is improving, but slang still confounds me.*

Daria glanced up at him with a playful smirk. She had easily noted his reaction to milk. She poured the hot milk into two large mugs. Steam rose from the mugs as she stirred carefully, wafting an intriguing aroma into the air. His mouth began to water in anticipation.

Daria blew gently and did a quick sample taste. She added a dash of another powder. With a satisfied nod and slow smile, Daria handed it carefully to Kairn.

He stared at the rich, dark brown liquid, curls of steam rising from the surface. He could not name the ingredients, but his nose twitched madly—swept joyfully under the truly wonderful wave of intoxicating scents.

He absently took a sip from his mug. He smiled as a cornucopia of new and complex flavors exploded on his tongue. It was rich, hot, and thick. The perfect blend of sweetness with just a hint of earthy bitterness. A sublime dash of spice. Bright herbal undertones.

He drained the large cup. He was neat, but he knew he had been very quick. Too quick for Fleet manners...by any standards.

He looked up, Daria was watching him with an indulgent smile, but unspoken heat simmered in her eyes.

Without a word, she topped off his cup with the remaining hot chocolate. Kairn smiled his thanks; he took a slow appreciative sip, savoring the decadent treat his Mate had shared with him. Daria saw his unspoken question and rattled off her litany of ingredients. "Whole milk. Liberal dashes of heavy cream."

She slanted a teasing brow at him and continued, "Dark unsweetened chocolate from Spain. Raw sugar. Pure extract of Vanilla. A few drops of peppermint oil. A few buds of dried lavender."

Daria blew gently and took a small sip, her eyes half closing. For long moments, Kairn stared...enthralled. Her voice was soft and intimate. "That packaged junk is an insult. *This* is hot chocolate."

As they shared the moment, Kairn knew he would forever associate his Mate with that small house and the decadent taste of hot chocolate.

CHAPTER TWENTY-THREE

Daria

Heart-meltingly gentle and patient. A lively sense of humor. A brilliant mind. A kind heart. Daria found him shockingly physically perfect. He was already maddeningly attractive, but Kairn without a shirt...she could get drunk on him. He was downright intoxicating.

Thick silver hair framed his strong-featured face. His tall ears peaked teasingly from his hair. His wide shoulders with the thick ruff of silvery fur that narrowed to a thick band along his spine. His chest with the smooth slide of muscles under a very light coat of fine short fur. Her favorite spot over his hearts. Her fingers fisted to keep from touching him.

Daria tugged the collar of Kairn's shirt high around her neck. She caught a whiff of his scent on the heavy material. She took a deep slow breath when he wasn't looking, the fading scents of spice and musk still making her heady. She was never giving it back, but she was going to have to get him to wear it again. As Kairn's eyes glowed hungrily, Daria didn't think he'd mind.

The rich flavor of hot chocolate lingered on her tongue. Daria couldn't look away from Kairn's eyes. Somehow, the simple act of sharing hot chocolate with Kairn felt crazily intimate. She felt his gaze drift over her. It felt like a touch. He set their cups down and wrapped his arm around her, taking care to tuck her close to his left side—close against his hearts. Daria felt an upwelling of tenderness. *He remembered.*

Daria tilted her head up and saw his eyes ignite. He lifted her up just as a cold wet nose pushed insistently against her leg. With a rueful laugh, Daria looked down to see Molly searching intently for the mugs.

Daria blew out a gusty sigh. She leaned back in Kairn's arms, felt the hunger in his tightly held muscles. Her lips parted as Kairn's head dipped toward her.

She distantly heard Molly bark in an indignant demand. With a sigh, Daria looked at an unrepentant Molly. As Kairn gently lowered her feet to the floor, Daria rolled her eyes in indulgent exasperation. "Bad girl...you have such bad timing."

Daria poured some milk in Molly's bowl. Kairn snorted, reluctant amusement lighting his eyes. "Not an adequately negative description. Horrid."

Daria shook her head. "Dreadful."

Kairn paused. "Devilishly inspired."

Daria shook her head sadly. "That's two words. No cheating. Diabolical."

Kairn quickly declared, "Lamentable."

Daria shared a quick grin with him. "Unfair advantage. You have a built in English dictionary. Machiavellian."

Kairn laughed in appreciation. "It is *your* native language. I deserve that head start. Nefarious."

Daria snorted. "Good one. Abominable."

Kairn looked at Molly happily lapping at the milk in her bowl. "Conspiracy."

Daria paused for a moment, looking at Molly licking the now empty bowl. "Maybe. I'm rewarding bad behavior."

Kairn had a tender smile on his face. "Delaying tactic. It is still your turn."

She drawled out, "Execrable."

Kairn leaned forward, staring meaningfully into her eyes. "Cockblocker."

Memories and electric awareness shimmered between them. Lost in the moment, they stared at each other. They dissolved into shared laughter. Deep understanding resonated between them. Daria had found her kindred spirit. One who followed her with hungry eyes. Remembered and acknowledged the little things that meant so much to her. Understood and engaged her often twisted sense of humor. Gave her the precious gift of time for them to learn each other.

Daria smiled to herself. *Recently, my life sounds like the plot of many current, popular romance novels. Kairn has declared himself mine openly. Frequently. Proudly. I am forever grateful that he had no concept of human political correctness. There is no uncertainty. I always know where I stand with him.*

Honor was deeply embedded in him. She had never given the word much thought before. *It seemed so easy...to do what you say. And say what you do. In reality, it is quite rare.*

Daria took a deep breath. *From this moment, I am going to trust my instincts and stop second guessing things. It might take baby steps, but I am going to claim him.*

CHAPTER TWENTY-FOUR

Kairn

Kairn helped Daria clean up. She disappeared briefly into the bathroom.

He heard water running. When she came back, she firmly put Molly up in the bedroom. She looked at him with clear, direct eyes. "I'm getting tired. I'm going to take a long bath."

Kairn nodded slowly, desperately trying to *not* think of Daria...naked...wet. His voice was hoarse. "I will await you out here."

She walked toward the bathroom. Her hand on the doorknob, she turned. He heard her take a deep breath. "Remember your tickling debacle. I haven't forgotten. You owe me a forfeit after your surrender."

Daria smiled slowly into his eyes. "I'd like you to join me."

Kairn blinked. Twice. Her expression was shy. It was also hopeful and determined. He leashed his savage flare of hunger. "Whatever you want. Only as far as you want."

He meant the reminder more for himself. He knew his eyes were glowing, but Daria smiled at his calm words. She looked back at him expectantly. He followed her into the cozy room. His eyes were fixed on the white oval...very inviting tub. It rested on whimsical clawed metal feet. It was unusually deep, high, and long.

Even he would be able to fit in it—though it would be a snug fit. Steam rose gently from the rapidly filling surface. Kairn quashed the tantalizing images flashing in his mind.

As the Water level rose swiftly, Kairn suppressed a wince as he realized the sheer volume of Water needed to fill the tub. Daria had a chastened look on her face. She turned the faucet off. It was nearly a third full. "I know it looks awful. It is a lot of water. It's collected rainwater filtered from my cisterns. It won't go to waste. It will be processed after we use it. It's stored and re-purposed into the beds of lavender."

Kairn felt his cock twitch uncontrollably when she said "rain." He grimaced and shook his head firmly, "You do not need to justify water for a bath. I do not mean to sound critical. Old habits. Space travel dictates careful water usage. In space, Water is a priceless commodity."

Daria said quietly, "It is here too. Humans, at least in America, are a bit spoiled. We have taken it for granted."

Their eyes met as they both considered the devastating events which had brought the Guardian to Earth. She lay her hand gently over his hearts and added, "Things may never get back to where they were, but they are improving. Some things on Earth may even be better. Because of you."

Daria leaned into his left side. "Let's enjoy our bath."

His hearts stopped, then thundered in his chest. Daria opened a glass jar and shook something into her hand. She sprinkled it into the water.

Dried blue flower buds floated on the water, the distinctive scent of lavender filling the steamy air. She lifted her fingers to his lips. "Taste..."

Kairn opened his mouth without hesitation. He felt her fingers brush ever so gently over his lips, grazing his tongue. He slowly licked a flower bud off her fingertips. A bright herbal flavor accented the taste of her skin. Meeting his glowing eyes, she lifted her same fingers. With a shy determined smile, she touched them to her lips, licking lightly. "This is lavender."

Her eyes fluttered. Warm rosy color swept upwards from her neck to her cheeks. "And you."

She slowly slid her pants off, baring her legs. All those curves. Kairn stared. He felt his canines start to lengthen. She took off some ridiculously small flimsy undergarment. Still staring, Kairn could smell a hint of her arousal in the air. She was now clad only in his shirt.

Daria paused with her fingers on the fastening. Kairn became aware of a constant low growling. He realized distantly that it was emanating from him. Daria looked into his eyes for long moments. Kairn saw trust and a growing, matching hunger in her steady gaze.

Her fingers slid the fastener down. Kairn saw the material loosen and swing open. Daria shrugged slightly. In slow motion, his shirt dropped to the floor. Revealing all that amazing smooth bare skin. Kairn struggled vainly to form a sentence.

Daria stood quietly with her shoulders back. He could see her pulse beating madly in her throat. Her breasts moved gently with her quick breaths; her nipples tight. The wicked curve of her hips, the scent of her arousal was now rich in the air.

With effort, Kairn subdued most of his growling. He reluctantly forced his eyes up. Met her shyly confident stare. He ground out, "Lovely. Truly."

Slowly, she eased closer and nestled her head into his chest. Into *her* spot. Kairn curved his arms around her. He could feel her breath warm his skin under the fine thin layer of his chest fur. She rubbed her head against him slowly. He felt shivers run through them both.

Kairn took a deep fortifying breath. He could count his pulse in the demanding ache of his cock. Sternly, he reminded himself that he had to leave the next morning. He wrestled for hard won control. He rumbled softly, "I have to be back at base camp in the morning."

He saw the uneasy questions in her eyes. Kairn knew he needed to explain how he felt to her. Even to his ears, it sounded jarring and awkward. For once, he wished he had the gift of eloquence. Kairn could not keep the growl out of his voice. "Never think this is a rejection. I will treasure this. You command every bit of my attention."

Kairn bared his hearts. "I wish to always serve you well. I want nothing more than to have us indulge in long lazy hours sharing the gift of ourselves with each other. Your first...our first time will not be under any time constraint. It is a celebration...And I cannot...I will not insult you by leaving mere hours after we share our bodies."

Kairn felt Daria press closer. Her voice was rich with tenderness, "You've spent a lot of time thinking about this."

Kairn laughed, low and intimate. "In wonderful aching detail. Drawn out anticipation...Pleasure will be all the better for it."

Daria was quiet. Her smile was touched with regret. "So...Either I'm under dressed, or you have some catching up to do."

Kairn hugged her close, dropping soft kisses on her nose and endearing pout. "Trust me, *Molindri*."

CHAPTER TWENTY-FIVE

Daria

Daria sighed, need still smoldering in her core. Her voice soft with tender amusement, she murmured, "I adore you for taking such sweet time...but you're going to kill me with foreplay."

He recoiled and leaned back. She heard Kairn's deep voice, suddenly harsh. "What is for play? And why would it kill you? I would never do anything to hurt you!"

She thumped her head against his chest in disbelief. "Did I actually say that aloud? Oh my God...Really?!"

Daria stared at him, blushing hotly. "I didn't...it's what..."

She took a deep fortifying breath. "Foreplay. One word...it's anticipation. Long...drawn...out...delicious anticipation."

She leaned back and started to slip out of his arms. "I'll get dressed..."

Kairn shook his head slowly. He took his comms off his wrist and set it on the sink. "I will master this English language so there are no misunderstandings between us."

He growled out. "Foreplay."

Kairn savored the word. He undid the fastener on his uniform trousers. "I would never deny you. I understand now. Foreplay is pleasure."

With mesmerizing fluid grace, he stripped out of them easily. "Sweetling, you will have your bath."

Daria caught a brief tantalizing glimpse of his long hard cock—the engorged head resting against the expanse of sharply defined abdominal muscles. Kairn swept her up in his arms and stepped down into the tub.

He carefully settled them both in the hot water, the scent of lavender in her nose. He lowered his head, his warm breath tickling her ear. "Tell me what you would do in a bath…"

Daria felt him kiss the shell of her ear gently. "I…uh…wash my hair."

She rubbed her head absently against his chest…heard the steady beat of his hearts. His voice was soft. "With what?"

Daria pointed. "Shampoo."

A few seconds ticked by. Daria could hear the soft rush of his breath and feel the heat of his stare. She heard the splash of water and felt warm water wet her hair. The soft snick of a cap. Daria heard him sniff. Kairn rumbled appreciatively. She heard soft sounds as Kairn coated his hands liberally with the rich liquid.

Daria felt his growl of pure appreciation vibrate deliciously through her. The familiar scent of chocolate tickled her nose. His large hands were warm, gentle…so decadently slow. He took his time as he worked the rich lather through her tousled strands. He stroked it from end to end, careful not to miss an inch of hair on her head.

She felt him scratching her head gently with carefully sheathed claws. Her head rolled bonelessly against him. Daria groaned softly. She could hear the smile in his voice as he murmured softly. "Yes?"

Daria barely suppressed a whine. "Please…don't stop."

Kairn cradled her head against his chest. She could feel the tenderness in his slow touch. His hands played softly in her hair…threaded gently through the strands until they lay flat and straight. Kairn massaged her head with slow lazy circles. Gentle firm pressure. Her body hummed in anticipation.

He dropped soft kisses along the curves of her ears as her head rolled restlessly. His strong fingers explored the tight muscles from the nape of her neck, the callouses scratching lightly and making delicate shivers ripple through her in exquisite response. The gentle slope of her shoulder. Long smooth strokes in a ruthlessly slow...thorough massage.

Over and over. Running his hands in long leisurely strokes from the curve of her collarbone to the tips of her fingers. Teasing the sensitive skin between each finger.

Daria felt his cock press hungrily between her thighs...sliding between her soft folds. Daria arched her hips back, restless and searching.

Kairn pulled soft ravenous groans from her. His cock stroked teasingly against her pussy. Kairn saturated her senses with the slow caress of his hands—contrasting with the escalating firm pressure of his cock against her pulsing swollen clit...until the spiraling tension deep in her core clenched hard and finally unraveled.

Daria felt Kairn press light kisses on her exposed nape. She heard him sniff deeply at her hair. His voice was soft. "I know lavender. What is this scent? It smells of you and that intoxicating drink you plied me with."

Daria smiled sleepily. Her body was still rippling with aftereffects of her pleasure. She tried to gather her thoughts, but still felt deliciously boneless and lethargic—in the very best possible way. Daria still wasn't capable of a sentence. She smiled slowly. "More...Chocolate."

She felt Kairn shift beneath her. The water was still warm, but his body burned with evocative heat all along her back. She could feel his cock press hotly against the small of her back. Her eyes widened in surprise. Her hips shifted over him instinctively. Her voice was soft.

"You didn't..."

She met his gaze as Kairn stared back at her. He smiled hungrily.

"Not yet. Foreplay."

His eyes alight with anticipation, Kairn lifted the bottle of shampoo with a deepening growl. "Rinse and repeat."

CHAPTER TWENTY-SIX

Kairn

After another round with that addictive shampoo, Daria had been near drunk with pleasure. Kairn reminded himself of the looming time constraints.

Kairn had gently washed every inch of her body; he took care to sooth her with light tender touches. He had dried her body and hair carefully with the long wide sheets of soft fluffy material he found hanging near the tub.

With a smile of pure appreciation, Kairn studied the delicate array of shampoo and soap bottles...noting, with a flare of heat, which ones he would have to acquire.

He had found her room easily by her unique fragrance. He argued fiercely with himself about putting her to bed but could not bring himself to leave her. That pretty little bed of hers would have snapped under half his weight.

He lay under her large window with the glass sculptures that seemed to beg for a touch. Kairn smiled. *I did not know the name then, but that was foreplay as well.*

Daria was deeply asleep, her body draped possessively...trustingly over his chest. He stared out at the dark sky. He knew the night would be long as the tempting scents of chocolate and lavender rose from her warm skin, invoking vivid memories of her soft cries of trust and need under his slow hands. Kairn smiled slowly. *I would not have it any other way.*

Kairn shuddered as pleasure pulsed through him. Daria sighed in her sleep, her warm breath ruffling the thin layer of fur on his chest. Her soft skin rubbed so softly against him with her every breath. He could still smell the dizzying scent of her arousal whenever her legs shifted. His cock throbbed in urgent painful demand. His seed pulsed slowly from the head and left a gleaming trail down his shaft.

Kairn could see the promise of their future. He stroked his hands gently over her. She shifted sleepily until she settled into her spot with a contented sigh, laying her head over his hearts.

Kairn felt them flutter as tenderness flooded through him. *She has learned to trust me. That is a gift I will forever treasure. I will not press her for more.*

Kairn let out a soft growl. *My pleasure belongs to her. I will not alleviate my need while she sleeps trusting and unaware beside me. Her pleasure. Our shared pleasure. It will be her choice. She needs to be awake and lucid to make her own decision.*

Kairn sniffed deeply at Daria's hair; her scent centered him. Their courtship was delicious. Daria was not aware of the precious gift she had already given him. He would prize the memories they made as the rare treasures they were. He felt his hearts slow to a steady beat. Kairn knew, with bone deep certainty, that Daria had already changed the course of his life in wondrous ways he could not fathom.

CHAPTER TWENTY-SEVEN

Daria

Daria stirred. She was incredibly warm. Her eyes opened to the grey light just before dawn. She stretched, feeling an exquisite ache...and woke to a flood of dizzying memories. Her firm bed lifted under her. She heard Kairn laugh softly.

She looked up slowly to meet the warm amusement in his eyes. His large hands cradled her neck, scratching her head gently. His voice was sweetly knowing. "You remembered."

Daria smiled tenderly. "You washed my hair."

Kairn smiled back gently. His eyes heated as they traced over her face in a nearly tactile caress. "I did. Twice. The bottle said rinse and repeat."

Daria leaned into his chest. They shared a soft laugh. Daria was quiet for long moments. "I've never...I felt..."

She felt herself blushing hotly. "I didn't know washing my hair could feel like that. It felt like so much more than that..."

Kairn dropped a soft kiss on her lips. She could feel the barely leashed hunger in his touch. His voice was quiet, but rich with feeling. "It was intimate because we made it so. When we share our inner selves...our Bond deepens."

Daria could feel his hard cock under her belly. Abruptly, she tried to lift her body away. "You didn't co...Am I hurting you? You've been hard for hours. Priapism...Human males can have permanent damage to..."

Daria stopped her frantic movements when Kairn shook his head calmly, holding her hips close to his. "Luperans do not have that issue."

He tilted his head as he accessed his translator. Wincing with empathy, Kairn added wryly, "Thankfully."

Daria chose her words. "With us, I feel like you're always giving to me...the flying lessons...washing my hair. I feel like I put you off. I feel guilty..."

Kairn's fingers tightened briefly before he relaxed them with obvious effort. His eyes flared in surprise—dulling with pain. Kairn's features tightened as he searched for words to explain. He shook his head fiercely. "There is no place for guilt between us."

His voice warmed. Daria could see the care he took in his words. She could hear the unadorned truth and feeling in his voice. "There is no keeping track of such things between us. You cannot know what you have given me. You are hope for the future I never knew I could have."

Kairn took her hand gently in his, eyes burning into hers. Kairn pressed her shaking fingers firmly to his long hard cock. He stroked their hands together up and down the length of his thick shaft.

Daria felt him shiver. His skin was hot and smooth. His flesh leapt eagerly under her gentle wondering touch—exquisitely responsive to her slightest touch. Vibrant. Alive.

His voice was a hungry growl. "There is no pain. This is only pleasure. This has not...will not happen in the presence of another being. Only ever you."

Kairn tried to lift their hands away, but Daria tightened her grip gently. She spoke softly. "Please. I want to touch you."

Silent, Kairn nodded slowly as his eyes glowed with a flare of heat. Her hand tentatively explored his cock, sliding tenderly along the sensitive length. Daria felt Kairn take a deep shuddering breath as her touch grew more confident...and became possessive. She could see...*feel* the beat of his hearts in the throbbing of his cock. Small pearls of his light blue seed slid down his shaft and coated her slowly stroking hand.

Daria groaned softly. She could feel the aching desire slick between her legs, the hot trail flowed down her inner thigh. Her other hand gently squeezed his large tight balls. She couldn't remember moving it there. Her hand slid up and down his engorged shaft, tracing the thick veins.

He was hard. Slick. Hot.

He sought her eyes, melding their gaze in an intimate embrace. Kairn's hips bucked as his cock thrust hungrily in her snug hold. Her hand slid faster up and down his throbbing cock. Over and over. His breathing was labored, his hearts thundering. He was groaning. Growling. His words were broken. "So...close."

Daria moved her hand faster, gently squeezing his balls. Kairn howled, his hips locking as long ropes of light blue seed shot from his throbbing cock. She stared raptly at his uninhibited response as he gloried in her touch. Daria felt pleasure wash through her as her core clenched in echoing spasms.

Daria collapsed onto his heaving chest. His hands had a faint tremor as he gently stoked through her tousled hair. Daria raised her hands to stoke over his hearts and paused. She was mesmerized by the warm thick seed still coating her fingers. Daria started to speak, but she paused. Looking over his sprawled body, her attention caught by the large opalescent pools gleaming temptingly on his hard belly.

Kairn followed her gaze. He hesitated for long moments, then reached out and snagged a towel discarded at his side. With dawning regret, Daria watched as he carefully wiped every trace of the silky fluid off each of her fingers. Before she could find her voice, Kairn had dried his belly with a few quick careless strokes and tossed the damp towel aside.

Kairn cradled her face gently and lowered his forehead to hers. Daria saw the raw hunger, need, and tenderness in his eyes. His breath slowly evened out. She could hear the pride in his voice as he fought to be gentle. "This is the desire only my Mate stirs in me."

With glad acceptance and hard-won understanding, Daria cuddled closer and gently corrected, "This is the joy we create. When we share the pleasure of our bodies."

She watched hope kindle in his eyes. Daria placed a careful hand over his racing hearts. Her voice was compelling...soft...sure. "Together."

CHAPTER TWENTY-EIGHT

Kairn

Kairn sat with his back propped against the wall and enjoyed the view outside the window. The sun had not yet risen. The sky was grey with the gathering storm clouds. Thunder sounded in the distance. Jagged streaks of lightning lit the horizon over the turbulent ocean. He could smell the promise of rain in the charged air. It was a beautiful morning.

Dozing lightly, Daria settled herself more comfortably across his lap. Kairn smiled as she shifted into her favorite spot with a contented sound. Daria rubbed her head absently over his hearts. They were in their own little world.

A soft chirp sounded from the bathroom. Kairn stirred reluctantly. He gathered Daria up, settling her gently on the deep-seated sofa. He drew a nearby blanket over her. He maneuvered a pillow carefully under her head. He grinned when she grumpily mumbled and turned over, still asleep.

Kairn padded quietly into the bathroom. He gave the bathtub a heated look, vivid images of what they had shared flashing through his mind. He spotted bottles on the bathing shelf. He opened the caps and sniffed.

Heat spiked in his blood as the familiar scents evoked powerful memories of their intimacy. He realized—with a tender smile—that they always would.

Kairn put most of them back in their place. He studied the remaining bottles with keen interest. They looked like toys in his large hand. He closed his fingers over them with care. *I will guard these like the little gems they are.*

Kairn took a modified comm link out of his pocket. He checked it with a nod of approval and replaced it. Absently securing his comm on his wrist, he read the report as he pulled his trousers on. He headed back to Daria but paused at a plaintive whine at the closed bedroom door. Kairn heard Molly yip. *Heard you out there. Can smell you. Let me out. Out.*

Kairn opened the door and nabbed an escaping Molly by her collar. He spoke as quietly as he could, "Keep quiet. Our Daria still sleeps."

Kairn walked to the front door, a now sedate Molly at his side. Kairn eased the door open, and Molly slipped out quietly. Shedding her decorum, the large shepherd exploded into a gallop as soon as her paws hit the grass.

Kairn turned back, shaking his head as Molly played chase with overly curious squirrels. It was obvious that the squirrels were running circles around the gleeful dog. A quick yip and bark, quickly stifled by a contrite Molly. *Almost there. Just a little closer.*

A daring squirrel darted across the path...and Molly was off again. Kairn made sure he could see Molly sprinting back and forth through the large window and shut the door very quietly.

Kairn heard Daria laugh softly. He looked up to see Daria watching him with a tender smile. She sat up, tucking her knees close to her chest to make room for him. Absently, Daria started to pat the cushion next to her. She glanced out the window. "Weather looks bad. Molly, strangely enough, loves storms."

Kairn looked askance at the sturdy-for-a-human sofa and sank instead to the floor next to her. With a rueful laugh, Daria joined him on the hardwood floor. She wriggled a bit trying to get comfortable.

Kairn raised an eyebrow and lifted his left arm in silent invitation.

Daria eased onto his lap; she snuggled against his hearts with a contented sigh.

Daria turned her head to look at him when his hard cock twitched against her spine. Her hips arched reflexively into him. She sent him a quizzical look over her shoulder. Her voice was intimate and warm. "You're...uh...hard again."

Kairn shrugged, ever present hunger simmering deep in his eyes. "These days, I usually am. I am like that whenever you touch me. When I think of you. When you smile. When I smell your unique scent. And I am glad of it."

Gentle humor tinged his tone. With hearts-felt satisfaction and a wicked smile, he said succinctly, "Basically, for me, everything about you is the most exquisite Foreplay."

CHAPTER TWENTY-NINE

Kairn

As the minutes passed, they basked in the simple joy of each other's company. Finally, Kairn knew it was time. His voice was heavy with regret, "I will have to leave for a briefing at base command."

Kairn got to his feet and eased Daria back on the sofa. Kairn's voice rumbled, "I have something to show you."

Kairn opened his hand and showed her the contents. Daria focused on the brightly colored glass and picked up the shampoo bottles. She opened one and sniffed at the evocative scent of dark chocolate.

Kairn was quiet while he watched her sniff at the containers. He said softly. "This and lavender are fast becoming two of my favorite scents."

With a mischievous smile, Daria asked. "What's your favorite scent?"

Kairn was solemn. "You."

Kairn heard her breath catch. His voice deepened into a growl. "And yours?"

Daria's voice was soft. "Us. Together."

Kairn cupped her face gently in his warm hands. His eyes made her a promise. Time was running short. Kairn shook himself out of his reverie. *I have to explain this.*

He looked at her seriously. "That's not what I wanted to show you."

He corrected himself. "Not the only thing."

Kairn slowly dropped his hands. His hands clenched to keep from reaching for her. He took a short step back and pulled the comm link out of his pocket.

Daria's voice was bemused. She accepted it with a bemused smile as she snapped it on her wrist. "You got me a comm link? So we can talk?"

Kairn frowned slightly. "In a manner of speaking. My comm is simplistic."

He pressed a small knob on his comm. "That tells the shuttle's computer to prepare for departure and do safety diagnostics."

Kairn said softly. "Your comm is keyed to your voice as primary. Tell it to display perimeter defense."

Kairn saw the startled look on Daria's face, but she echoed his words. "Display perimeter defense."

A holographic display deployed from her comm link and detailed her cottage, meadow, tree line, and coastline. A calm female voice intoned, "Force fields at capacity. Perimeter extends 100 Earth meters into forest line, over the water, and elevation above current domicile. Current settings allow entry and exit of documented native fauna. Program recognizes one Daria Morrissey and canine fauna Molly. Program accepts authorized entry/exit of current air and land transport on site. Under emergent conditions, program recognizes default Kairn, Commander of Alliance warship Guardian. Current force field capability is above Alliance standard. It will repel any attack —even exceeding maximum power armament currently in use by the Alliance."

With resignation and rising trepidation, Kairn watched Daria turn to him with wide eyes. "This is what you were doing in my forest yesterday!"

Kairn shook his head. "I was upgrading the system. Breis, my head engineer, designed the force field and modified the comm link. I set the original perimeter guard when I followed you home the first time you had time off."

Daria was silent. He could see the rapid flow of thoughts and emotion on her expressive face. Her voice was sharp. "If you were an Earth male, I would find these things alarming. Stalker-ish. Humans report this behavior to the police."

She clarified, "Local law enforcement."

Daria stared sternly at him. Kairn could not suppress his faint flinch and knew Daria saw the telltale sign.

Kairn watched as a lovely rush of rosy color suddenly warmed her cheeks. Daria's voice softened. "But I remember. You're not from Earth. You're protecting me..."

Kairn felt his features settle into a ruthless expression. He could feel his eyes glowing and his canines lengthen. He ground out fiercely, "It is my nature to protect my Mate. Every time. By whatever means necessary. Even if I know you will not like it. Your safety is paramount...every time."

Daria was quiet for a long moment, a soft smile beginning to tug at her lips. "Well, I'll always know what you've done and why. You surely don't mince words."

Digesting her words, he arched an eyebrow. Her smile widened and sweetened. "You're honest...even if you didn't have to be. There's an expression that fits you perfectly. Ask forgiveness, not permission."

She laughed ruefully, "I can't fault you for that. It's what I'd do... what I will do."

Daria stared at him meaningfully, her eyes warm. "Protection is how you show your feelings and Bond for me. I get it."

Daria leaned over and rested her hand on his steady hearts. "I trust you."

Kairn leaned down and sniffed contentedly at her hair. *She understood. She stands her ground. She concisely argued her point. My Mate. I am so proud of her.*

He heard her mumble into his chest, an odd note of humor in her voice. "When you do things like that...we have to talk."

Kairn shook his head in amusement. It must be more Earth slang. He would ask her the non-literal meaning later.

CHAPTER THIRTY

Daria

His comm pinged sharply. Kairn took a slow step back, reluctance in every line of his big body. His voice was quiet. "I need to leave."

He reached down to the floor and snagged something. Kairn shook it out and Daria recognized his uniform shirt. He shrugged into it. Daria dressed quickly in a light T-shirt and yoga pants. Daria walked past the door. He paused abruptly. "What is amiss?"

Daria's eyes wandered down his body, drawn by the flashes of his hard flesh teasing her between the gaping sides of the shirt. She forced her eyes back up to his face. "Nothing. Everything is actually really good. I'm going back with you."

Kairn frowned slightly. "You are supposed to use this time to recuperate. I do not think base command will be a particularly restful environment for you."

Daria smiled slightly. "I've had enough rest. I'd like to spend more time with you. If you don't think I'll be a distraction."

Daria winced at her choice of words. "As long as you don't mind."

She did a mental eye roll at herself. *That was no better!*

Kairn strode out the door and waited until Daria locked it. He swept her up and moved at a rapid clip across the wide meadow.

Karin ran in silence for a while. She could hear the warm reassurance in his voice when he finally spoke. "You are welcome all the time. Whenever possible, I want you with me."

His arms cradled her a little closer. "You are a distraction, but not in the way you think."

He hesitated briefly, his voice soft and intimate. "I am always aware of you. It is a good thing. A very good thing."

Daria let his words soak into her hungry heart. She tucked her head against his hearts and relaxed. His gait was smooth as silk. The scenery was a blur. Daria whistled for Molly. Glancing back, she saw a hazy Molly-shaped form galloping at full speed far behind them.

Daria blinked when they arrived at the shuttle. She had just barely settled in to enjoy her ride. It was easily 1.5 miles to the clearing where the shuttle rested. Kairn's breathing was easy. He glanced behind them. "We will have to wait for Molly."

Daria watched as Kairn checked fuel stores. He plotted the coordinates to base command. He synch'd his comm to the shuttle's onboard computer. She smiled in affectionate approval. He was an excellent multitasker.

He absently started to seal his shirt fastener. Daria stood to touch his shoulder and found herself looking a good bit up at the tail end of his shoulder blade.

She shook her head in bemusement. He was an absolute beast of a male with beautifully carved and proportioned musculature. He had the long, sharp teeth and claws of a born predator. He towered over her and she felt...wonderfully safe and protected.

Molly jumped into the shuttle with a scrabble of her paws. She flopped dramatically onto the cool metal floor, tongue lolling and panting heavily. Kairn turned to look at her as he started to tuck the shirt-tails into his trousers. Molly barked in escalating tones, punctuated with a shrill yip.

Daria drawled. "And..."

Kairn had a solemn look on his face. "Molly thinks my legs are too long."

Daria snorted. "Ain't that the truth! Molly, I feel your pain."

Kairn's lips quirked. "Daria, you cannot comment since you had a ride. Molly says I had an unfair anatomical advantage. In short...I cheated."

Kairn leaned over Molly and whispered loudly, "You need to get more exercise."

Molly flicked her ear dismissively. The big shepherd snorted, turning her nose up with disdain and settled down for a nap.

CHAPTER THIRTY-ONE

Daria

Kairn shut the doors to the shuttle and lifted off. He watched the sensors closely. Her comm pinged and announced, "Leaving perimeter of force field. Automatic defenses initiated."

Daria had been too excited to look around much on the trip up. She explored the surprisingly spacious shuttle. She watched Kairn set the auto pilot. He was now at the comm unit in an animated discussion. Deep in her body, heat stirred at his growling bass tones and the sleek strength visible in his broad muscled shoulders. She smiled, feeling a ready blush rise with the rush of memories.

Daria thought about the last few weeks. The last incredible day. They already knew so much about each other. She felt like she'd known him for years. She laughed a little when she remembered her awkward reaction to the first time he declared his feelings. *Thank God Kairn was so persistent. He'd had enough faith for us both.*

The comm clicked off. Daria absently rolled the small bottles in her hand with a soft clink. His large ears tipped back alertly and he turned to her. His expression was heated and predatory. He took a deep sniff. "We will need more of that. In much larger bottles."

Daria smiled even as she felt another blush. Crossing to her with fluid grace, Kairn brushed her cheek with a sweet lingering touch. "I like this color change on you. You do it when you feel...or remember pleasure. It lets me know I have done something you like."

Kairn's hand moved and gently scratched her head with barely-there touches of his careful claws. He stated softly, "You enjoyed the hair washing."

Daria's answer was half strangled. She groaned as he started to massage her nape with gentle hands.

"Beyond words, sweetheart."

She sighed. "Don't be surprised. I'll be asking you to shampoo my hair every chance we get...and scratch my head."

Daria felt Kairn kiss her hair softly and nuzzle deeply into the tumbled waves. He growled softly, "My pleasure. Why do you call me sweetheart?"

Daria turned her head and kissed his wrist. "It's my pet name for you. Because you are. Honey fits too because you're warm and sweet."

She saw his quick answering smile as his eyes glowed softly down at her. His hands paused as he massaged Daria's shoulder. She groaned. "No...don't stop. That feels so good."

Kairn's fingers resumed their bewitching slow circles. The quiet in the shuttle was only broken by Daria's occasional soft sigh or low groan. Daria was pretty sure she probably whined at several points.

In a pleasurable daze, Daria heard Kairn say, "Shampoo is a strange word. It is a vastly pleasurable shared experience. Why do you name it manufactured waste?"

He paused, considering. "Artificial excrement is another alternative."

Kairn tilted his head quizzically. He added dryly, "Neither one sounds nearly as pleasurable as it truly is."

Daria blinked...*Surely not.*

She turned her head to look at him. His eyes calm, Kairn looked at her expectantly as his hands continued to work their magic. *Oh yes.. he did.*

Graphic images assaulted her brain. Daria looked at the bottles of NEVER TO BE CALLED shampoo AGAIN in her hands. *Oh...fuck*

NO! I have extremely fond...intimate memories of them. Which we are going to add to again...and often.

A woman on a mission, Daria sat up and set about meticulously peeling the labels off. Every single tiny, sticky loathsome fragment. Daria stared at the innocuous tightly wadded ball of paper in her palm. She snickered, then snorted...and started laughing. She doubled over until tears ran down her face.

Finally calm, Daria said with a meaningful, fond glare at a puzzled Kairn, "You're right."

Her voice dripped with utter distaste. "This is not *shampoo*. We will never use that poor unfortunate word again. From now on...This is...hair soap..."

Daria made a face. "That didn't sound right."

She nodded briskly. "Hair wash...much better. I can deal with that."

Kairn leaned down and kissed her hungrily, his tongue teasing hers as it thrust slow and deep. Daria bit gently on his lower lip. He lifted his head slowly and growled out, "I adore the sound of your laughter. I also like hair washing very much. We will share both often."

Daria looked at Kairn with a wide smile. She knew her hair would be cleaner than it had ever been.

She let out a blissful sigh. *What a wonderful thing to be able to look forward to...and share. I can hardly wait.*

CHAPTER THIRTY-TWO

Kairn

The navigational computer beeped softly. Kairn switched the shuttle back to manual control. The temperature on the base was surprisingly cool. He touched the shuttle down with a soft thump in the busy landing area.

As the shuttle door opened, a wall of cold air rushed in. He looked at Daria and saw the shiver she tried to hide. With a sweet smile, Kairn took off his shirt and draped it carefully over her shoulders.

They were greeted by his openly gawking senior officers. The bright lights illuminated the many ships being attended to by the flight crew... and glinted off the very distinctive insignias denoting his rank with every movement Daria made.

There was a raucous flurry of affectionately derogatory comments in colorful Luperan—particularly on the painful spectacle he subjected them to with his bare chest and flagrant display of his charms.

Industrious mechanics passed briskly between craft, stealing not-very-subtle glances at his startled and very curious Mate. Kairn tucked Daria close to his side. He snarled in Luperan, "I am sure we will find an outlet for your excess energy. We will see about my vaunted charms in the sparring ring! Did you regress into a gaggle of untried, mannerless striplings without me to keep you in line? Make use of your translators. I know you heathens have been practicing. Speak English!"

A collective groan rose from his old friends. Kairn kept a warm hand at Daria's waist. He glowered at his grinning crew behind Daria's head. He kept introductions brief. "Daria Morrissey, these are my senior bridge crew...and my oldest friends."

He rattled them off concisely.

"Darzik, science officer and XO."

His old friend sniffed discreetly as he walked over and eyed him sharply in pleased surprise.

"Breis, engineering."

"Kirov, medical."

"Lirinx, security.

His officers all nodded politely. They were making a credibly valiant attempt to curb their inveterate curiosity. Ears tilted attentively forward, they were maintaining a very respectable distance.

Kairn was the first in their group to find his Mate. He knew that his discovery of his Daria so unexpectedly nurtured the long dormant seed of hope in them.

They knew better than to touch his intended.

Even among his trusted friends, they understood that his instinct to protect her was straining at his self-control. His usual air of unflappability was whisper-thin and could shatter with little provocation.

Kairn heard a nearly soundless thud as Molly jumped lightly out of the shuttle. The dog walked calmly between his large (even for Luperans) officers. Molly sat neatly at Daria's side, looking around with an air of studied nonchalance.

Daria laughed. "And...attitude is everything."

His officers proceeded ahead of them at a brisk pace to give them the illusion of privacy. Daria spoke in a carrying voice, "Just so you know...I'm keeping your shirt."

With a knowing smile, she leaned back and nuzzled her cheek into his chest. Kairn watched in stunned silence as Daria then sniffed delicately at his shirt...pointedly and repeatedly. Her voice was teasing. "Sweetheart, you'll have to wear this shirt for me later. It won't do me any good if it doesn't have your scent."

There was dead silence, and then the howls of his friends' delight-ed laughter floated back to them.

Kairn stared at Daria. She had just publicly and proudly claimed him. In no uncertain terms. Freely offered indisputable proof of her sweet acceptance. His hearts leapt.

CHAPTER THIRTY-THREE

Daria

Daria sat in the back of the meeting room, enjoying the easy repartee between her new Family. Kairn never had bothered to put a shirt on. His friends were having a field day. Kairn tolerated their teasing well.

Even she could identify the distinctive new note in his masculine scent. The sweet herbal bite of lavender was obviously teasing their sensitive Luperan noses.

Out of the eye of the human public, rank fell by the wayside. The easy camaraderie and rambunctious laughing banter between the old friends was a thing of beauty.

Darzik pulled up holograms. "These are the details on the Ichori worm hole generators. NOT, unfortunately, their latest design. These are my drafts of what the Ichori prisoners of war described. They said there was rumor of smaller versions which might be able to be deployed planet side."

A ripple of controlled concern flickered on all their faces. Kairn bit out shortly, "Details."

She watched Kairn and Darzik closely examine the images. Breis started brainstorming probable safeguards. Kirov and Lirinx observed the likely obstacles and put together the Luperan version of an emergency tool kit.

Daria tried to be unobtrusive, but she noticed Kairn's eyes did touch on her at wonderfully regular intervals. And lingered. There was a quiet pride and tenderness in his gaze. She lifted his shirt collar when she thought he wasn't looking and took a surreptitious, slow deep breath. Out of the corner of her eye, she saw a sweet, wondering smile curve his lips.

Daria smiled to herself. *Since when am I ever subtle? I'm sure not about to start now.*

Daria buried her nose in his shirt collar and took a deep satisfying sniff. His scent...their blended scent...flooded her senses and she flashed back to their bathtub.

Daria felt a surge of heat deep in her core. Kairn's head whipped around to look at her. His nostrils flared as his eyes glowed with a wonderfully familiar heat.

His voice was a barely audible growl. "We are done here. Prep two teams with full gear—Darzik, pull the recon assault armor you and Breis worked on. Comm me when you have the data from the new sensors and when the ships are ready."

At Kairn's order, his crew had gone collectively quiet and expectant. With a smiling glance at Kairn, Darzik paused to collect Molly. The room rapidly emptied. The door closed with a quiet snick as the lock engaged behind them.

Kairn prowled toward her with predatory grace, but his eyes were gentle. He sat next to her. His voice was somber. "I do not trust my control if others were to scent your arousal."

Kairn trailed his fingers down her cheek and cupped her jaw gently.

Daria could feel inherent hunger in his lingering touch. His eyes met hers. "We are exquisitely sensitive to each other. It is a response I value beyond description or measure. I find I am possessive and overprotective. When we share intimacy, it is for no one but ourselves."

Daria leaned into his warm bare chest, the fine layer of silky fur tickling her nose. She nuzzled until she found her spot. She heard

Kairn's breath catch. He cuddled her closer against his hearts with gentle hands.

Daria reached up and brushed her lips gently against his in a tender caress. She could feel his lips curving into a smile. She found the feel and taste of his smile intoxicating and addictive. Her lips lingered and clung, learning the curves of his.

He growled low and deep, the vibration in his chest shaking her body. "My Mate."

His lips brushed hers over and over. His teeth caught her lower lip and nibbled gently. Until she groaned with growing hunger and nipped his lip sharply. He growled, his tongue tracing her lower lip and then slowly slid deep into her mouth.

Daria shifted her hips in restless hunger; heated moisture slicked her core. She heard Kairn groan lowly as she slid over his hard cock. Kairn moved her legs so that she straddled him. Daria moved against his hard body. His hips bucked in helpless response. Their eyes met and held; his eyes glowed a bright, hot gold.

His comm pinged, the sound loud and intrusive. Kairn's head fell forward and then lifted slowly. His body was still tight with hunger, but his voice was warm with rueful humor. "By any chance...Is Molly here?"

There was a pregnant pause while Daria stared at him. She giggled, then snorted...and they dissolved into shared laughter. Daria managed to gasp out, "Cockblocker."

CHAPTER THIRTY-FOUR

Kairn

Kairn arched an inquisitive eyebrow at Daria and loosened his arms. Daria frowned slightly and nuzzled deeper into his embrace. His arms tightened around her precious weight.

His comm pinged with an incoming message. Over the comm, Kairn could hear the abject apology in Darzik's voice. "My pardon, brother. I would not have interrupted if it were not so pressing a problem."

Kairn took a deep fortifying sniff of Daria's hair. *She has become, unbeknownst to her, my anchor. She smells like home.*

Kairn answered calmly, his voice tinged with wry amusement. "I know you must have found something of considerable interest."

Darzik continued, a note of worry roughening his deep tones. "Most recent sensors have detected some discrepancies in the expected data. Water levels are rising. The air temperature is dropping...But both at slower rates than I would like. Or expect."

Kairn said thoughtfully, "The Ichori gave up considerable resources when they retreated from the planet. They may be making a second run here. We are going to do some recon. We will not have enough time to adequately brief the teams. To ensure familiarity with the new intelligence, we will have to split our bridge crew between them. Darzik, you are with me. Lirinx and Breis will head the other team."

Daria

Darzik was piloting the armored transport. Despite her considerable size and weight, the transport was moving at an impressive speed. Daria looked around at the tightly packed cabin. It was full of quietly confident Luperan warriors—all armed to the teeth with an arsenal of weapons she couldn't begin to fathom.

Kairn had planned to leave her at the command base. Daria had maintained (OK...argued) that the heavily armored transport would be better protected than the command base. Because...armor. In addition to a full complement of heavily armed Luperans. And a fiercely over-protective Kairn.

It had taken a lot of persuasion, but he had eventually conceded that she had a valid point. Daria smiled softly. If it were up to Kairn... she'd be accompanied by equally overprotective guards if he wasn't able to be there himself. She adjusted the comm on her wrist with an affectionate, rueful smile.

An insistent beep brought Kairn to the comms unit. His eyes brightened. "I have been expecting this report."

His lips quirking with quiet satisfaction, he arched a brow at Daria who had dropped bonelessly into a chair. "Would you like to see the progress your planet is making? I would like your input. We have no topography from before the attacks for comparison."

Daria hurried over to the console. She leaned into the hollow he provided when he lifted a welcoming arm. Kairn pulled up the hologram. He pointed out multiple points.

Daria leaned closer. "I'm not a weather specialist or a geologist, but there's no temperature gradient at the poles. There should be large continents covered in sheets of ice. And the temperature should be subzero."

Kairn called out the coordinates to Darzik. Outside images blurred as the ship picked up speed. When he turned, his voice was colder than she'd ever heard it. "I will set you down in the next secure city. It will be safer for you. The Guardian does routine sweeps. They have all been clean, but I do not know what we will find up there. The Ichori may well have other tech—like the wormhole devices—that we have difficulty sensing with our current equipment."

Daria blew out an angry breath. "You've told me that you're mine when I'm ready. You're not mine only when it's convenient! I'm going with you."

Kairn turned, his thin veneer of calm splintering. Raw emotion resonated in his voice. "I do not know what is out there. You are not a soldier. I will not have you at risk. I am yours."

His eyes were wild. More quietly, he finished. "I will not survive without you. I cannot...and I would not want to."

She saw the anguish he couldn't camouflage in his eyes. Daria felt a surge of empathy but reasoned softly. "Your ship is well armored. I've seen you check the shields and the weaponry. The guns are fully charged. We have a cabin full of fighters. You and Darzik are both excellent pilots. This is not an unreasonable choice. I'll just be an extra medic. You know full well that you can never have enough medics."

She laid a gentle hand over his hearts. "Whatever this is between us...I don't understand how or why, but I do know that you're mine. I'm yours."

She exhaled loudly. "What do you think it would do to me if I lost you? This connection...our Bond works both ways. You make me stronger. I will be careful and listen to your instructions. I won't do anything reckless. We're better together. You've asked me to trust you. Let me be your partner. You have my trust, Kairn. Trust me too."

He stared, their harsh breathing the only sound breaking the silence. "*Molindri.* You make very valid points. You are astounding. And honor me. We will go together."

CHAPTER THIRTY-FIVE

Daria

The transport was making good time; they were nearly to the North Pole. Daria fingered the scale-like uniform Kairn had given her just in case. This was their elite reconnaissance unit armor. It was surprisingly lightweight. It allowed easy movement and was deceptively supple. It was sized for the massive Luperans, but somehow adjusted to her body as she put it on.

Kairn had given her a quick overview. In short, it absorbed any energy blast and redirected it into fueling an essentially impenetrable shield—while somehow letting her fire her weapon. *Huh. Still can't figure that one out.*

And deadly accurate with the assistance of the weapons computer. It had been keyed to her vitals and shifted color/temperature to match her surroundings if she had an adrenaline surge.

She felt a wholly inappropriate surge of excitement. She had grown up watching Star Trek reruns and now she was a chameleon with her own personal force field. *Their tech was AMAZING!*

Daria snapped out of her reverie. She snickered to herself. *My fangirling!*

She glanced up to see Kairn watching her indulgently. They shared a warm smile. His smile faded as he checked the sensors and called out pertinent information to Darzik. "The sensors have found a source of intense heat. The continent is covered with ice, but it is much thinner than what you described. The Ichori probably left a device to melt the ice so they could pump the run off through a wormhole. It will likely be unstable and could close at any time."

Darzik landed the transport in short order. As the recon team gathered their gear, Darzik gripped Kairn's shoulder in passing. Before Darzik left, he ran a jaundiced eye over Daria's armor.

After they were alone, Daria sent Kairn a speaking glance. She heard him swallow a snarl as he ground out, "My instinct is to have you stay here where the transport can shield you. I left you an open comms line if we need it. I am leaving four of my best recon fighters with you. I have faith in you. I know you are a strong, capable wonderful female. I know you want to come with me."

Kairn traced the line of her jaw with light reverent fingers. Daria leaned into his hand; she basked in the tenderness inherent in his touch. Kairn's voice deepened as his eyes half closed. "Understand that, capable though you are, you are also mine. My instinct will run rampant. I will be consumed with the need to protect you. We can ill afford the slightest distraction. Any misstep could prove catastrophic for your Earth. You have done your job...and done it well. This is mine."

Daria nodded and managed a smile as he swept her into a feverish brief embrace. She felt his great hearts thrum under her ear.

The transport touched down and the ramp lowered with a quiet snick. His jaw brushed over her hair in a parting caress. His eyes darkening with grim determination, he stepped away from her and slung a large energy rifle over his shoulder.

Her voice hoarse, Daria called out. It was an order. "We have only just found each other, sweetheart. Come back to me."

Kairn closed his hand slowly into a fist over his hearts. He answered solemnly, "Always."

It was his promise as he turned and strode onto thin melting sheets of ice of the North Pole where his team was assembling.

CHAPTER THIRTY-SIX

Kairn

As Kairn exited the shuttle, Darzik skewered him with a horrified glare. Kairn shot Darzik a meaningful look. His voice was calm. "Enough, brother. It is worth it. You try to hide it, but I have seen your face when you are on a certain protective detail. Above all others, you should well understand my choice."

The two advance scouts stealthily slid back over the icy hill. The constantly adjusting camouflage of their armor adjusted to each minute change. They blended seamlessly into the terrain. The customized visual feed on his helmet was the only reason Kairn could see them.

Kairn murmured to Darzik, "Remind me to tell Lirinx he has trained his teams well. Breis did outstanding work adapting the armor and helmets."

His soldiers' faces were grim. "Commander, the Ichori have established a worm hole on the planet. They are melting the ice and loading harvesters. Approximately 1.5 Earth miles away. There are some large ice hills we can use as cover as we advance. There are ten Ichori soldiers that I laid eyes on guarding the base. They are posted in paired positions. They are all wearing eye protectors against the light. We were not detected, but the Ichori remain very vigilant."

Kairn nodded curtly. "Nicely done. It would have been suspiciously easy if they did not have the protectors."

He nodded slowly at his warriors. "We will just have to do this the hard way. That small a force is not typical of the Ichori. They may not anticipate their presence being discovered on the planet...or it may be a trap."

Kairn added quietly, "Keep half of your men in paired snipers on the high ground, one pair to each Ichori guard unit. Have them make sure there are not any unpleasant surprises. The rest of us will encircle the laser and the wormhole to minimize any further Water loss. Watch where you step. They can not see us in this armor, but they will see our prints in the melting snow...and be able to track us."

The teams separated, stealthily making their way toward the enemy camp. The ice covering the ground was softer with the planet's warmer temperatures. Their approach was both time consuming and exhausting—an exercise in frustration as they tried to camouflage their tracks. The Ichori soldiers were in the bottom of a bowl with steep, slick walls where the ice had been melted. The heat from the large lasers was turning the previously solid ground into a treacherous bog. Their faces grim, Ichori slogged through the heavy mud. Their large bodies sank to their knees with each step.

Large cumbersome harvesters rested heavily on the thawing ground; deep indentations adjacent to them on either side were daunting proof that many had already left. The wormhole was pulsating like an insatiable parasite.

Objectively, the Ichori were an impressive race. Resembling the dragons of old Earth lore, they were approximately ten Earth feet in height. They had nearly impenetrable scales in varying shades of bronze. Their forepaws were tipped with sharp curved talons.

They had what appeared to be fully functional wings, the points of which ended in sharp serrated spikes. Because of their sheer mass, they could glide from high ground; thankfully, no one had yet to see them actually *fly*. Kairn grimaced with reluctant admiration. *They are equipped with enough natural weapons. Formidable enemies already, I am glad they do not have that one in their armamentarium as well.*

They had heavy plating over their vital organs and their heads. The only safe way to kill an Ichori was from a distance with a double shot through the upper torso...one to penetrate the plating, one to burn through the heart.

The Ichori lived in deep caverns on their native planet; their one exploitable weakness was sensitivity to light. Aware of that vulnerability, the Ichori all sported protective lens. Typically, it would take at least eight elite Luperan warriors to defeat one Ichori in close combat.

Historically, close quarters combat with the Ichori never ended well. The Ichori practiced highly selective breeding in the never-ending pursuit of the perfect killing machines

An Ichori boarded a glutted harvester. He ponderously piloted it through the edges of the worm hole. Kairn signaled the teams. The sizzling sound of ten plasma heavy weapons discharged, with a second salvo nearly on top of the first. The Ichori targets dropped with synchronized heart shots.

Two unusually large (even for them) Ichori soldiers charged out of an idling harvester, their wings spread wide. Slogging determinedly through the sucking mud, Kairn led his warriors on the ground in a grueling race against the Ichori,

With unexpected speed, the Ichori bounded over to the lasers, tapping madly at the controls. The snipers fired repeatedly at the rapidly moving targets, connecting with one of the remaining Ichori. An automated voice on the large lasers intoned in Common Galactic, "Self-destruct activated."

The last Ichori blocked the way to the lasers, slashing and stabbing indiscriminately at the attacking Luperans. The Ichori's talons dripped freely with blue Luperan blood. Panting heavily, the Luperans fell back to regroup. As they caught their breath, the countdown inexorably ticked down.

Kairn ground out to his remaining soldiers, "Standard immobilization technique."

Kairn nodded at Darzik. They had fought together long enough to anticipate each other's attack moves. The Luperans attacked. Darzik slashed at the back of Ichori's knees and swept his legs out from under him. Ignoring the burning lacerations inflicted by the Ichori's talons, Kairn swarmed up the Ichori's heavily armored torso.

Kairn slashed the eye protectors to pieces with his claws. The Ichori screamed in agony, finally distracted as the weak sunlight hit his bared vulnerable eyes. The arrival of the Luperan snipers turned the tide. With the momentum of their charge down the icy hillside, they pinned the Ichori's massive limbs to the ground, four on each limb and wing.

The Ichori flailed wildly until he was secured with reinforced magnetic cuffs and sedated heavily. Kairn and Darzik looked the lasers over as the countdown continued with merciless efficiency.

Kairn ordered his warriors to pilot the remaining harvesters away to salvage the water. He posted the rest of his angrily protesting Recon team at a safe distance—just in case the inherently unstable worm hole imploded.

He signaled Lirinx and Breis with a crisp sit-rep of what to look for when they reached the southern pole. The meeting earlier that day meant they were the only ones who had an inkling of the ugly potential in the smaller inherently unstable wormhole.

Darzik sent an exhausted look at Kairn. "I hope this fledgling resistance movement of the Ichori takes hold."

Kairn grimaced in weary acknowledgement as Darzik carefully prised open the panel of the laser. Kairn saw the rapid swelling in Darzik's dominant hand from the battle. Nudging his old friend aside, Kairn answered gruffly, "Let us get to work and depart this place of evil humors."

Kairn stared into the small compartment and located the energy source. Stripping off his armored gauntlets, his large claws flexed involuntarily. He wished, for the first time, for smaller hands. He sent a prayer to his Gods for Daria.

Kairn met Darzik's grim eyes. Eyeing Kairn with foreboding, Darzik muttered fiercely, "Do not make me have to explain any mishaps to your Mate. As you are of her, she is just as fiercely protective of you. She will have my head!"

Kairn grinned proudly at the thought of his Mate. His smile faded as he concentrated on the delicate task before him. With excruciating care, he eased the tips of his smallest claws around the power crystal. Kairn simultaneously pulled both it and disarmed the self-destruct. The rushing sound from the steam roiling in choking clouds cut off in a moment of welcome silence. He blew out a shaky breath...

The wormhole abruptly collapsed on itself and the backlash threw them into the path of the Ichori machine as it blew apart in the wind-storm.

Kairn thought he heard muffled shouts in the distance. Sharp pain rolled over him in waves—followed by a blessed numbness. His vision dimmed. *Forgive me, Daria...I am trying my very best to keep my promise. I am so sorry, Molindri...*

He thought he heard Daria screaming his name as he was sucked under.

CHAPTER THIRTY-SEVEN

Daria

Daria turned away from the comm station. She adjusted the sensor readout in her helmet and checked the comms again. *Still nothing...*

The four warriors stationed themselves in protective positions around the transport. She could not read anything in their stoic faces. Time was crawling by and she hadn't heard from Kairn nor from anyone in his unit.

A loud boom sounded. The shuttle rocked. She was flung against the wall. Daria landed hard on the metal floor as the transport was racked by tremors. Something collided violently with the outer hull of the ship.

A section of the metal ceiling broke loose and fell with a dull clang. The heavy weight glanced off her helmet and landed on her mid back, securely pinning her in place. Lights flickered wildly and alarms blared.

Daria called softly, "Kairn."

Over and over again. She couldn't raise Kairn on comms. She heard several male voices answer her—urging her to remain calm. The door was crushed on one side. Metal screeched in protest as the door was forced open. From her limited vantage point, she smiled as large booted feet gathered around her. The heavy debris was carefully lifted off her.

Daria nodded gratefully to the grim males as they helped her to her feet. A gruff male asked, "Are you injured?"

Her voice was measured and calm despite the panic trying to sweep her under. "Just shaken. Are any of you?"

Daria made a concerted effort to keep her voice steady. "Have you heard from Kairn? Darzik?"

One of the soldiers, a grizzled veteran, stepped forward with quiet authority. With a speaking look, he silently directed the rest to walk the perimeter around the battered transport. "No, ma'am. To both questions."

He tapped his armor with a meaningful look. "We have these. We have notified the base. Reinforcements are en route. ETA 3 minutes. They are also prepping Med Evac."

Daria headed outside. "We need to search for them."

The soldier blocked her way. His voice was stern. "My orders are very clear. We are to protect you."

With steely determination, Daria really looked at the soldier for the first time. "There is no choice. That is my Mate out there. Your brothers-in-arms. You won't...can't stop me."

CHAPTER THIRTY-EIGHT

Daria

It seemed to have taken an eternity. Reinforcements had arrived. They were still searching the rough terrain for Kairn and his team.

Daria stumbled nearly blind through the smoke and steam. A hoarse shout rang out, "Here. Over here!"

Daria sprinted over the uneven ground, strewn with twisted pieces of metal. She fell to her knees at Kairn's side. He was barely conscious but flailing wildly. His features nearly unrecognizable with anguish, Darzik knelt with grim determination over Kairn's prostrated form.

Darzik was pale, his multiple lacerations dripping blue blood onto Kairn's body. Darzik was struggling to hold him down. The field medic was desperately sweeping over Kairn's body with the portable cryogen unit.

Daria's voice was high and thin. "Kairn...sweetheart. We've got you. Hang on."

His eyes focused on her briefly and warmed in recognition. A weak smile flickered on his lips.

Daria put a gentle hand on his chest, barely touching him. "Sweetheart, I need you to be still so the medic can do his job."

At the minute pressure of her hand, he stopped struggling. His eyes locked on her. She was his lodestone.

Daria assessed him rapidly. His armor was charred and studded with shrapnel, shredded badly in places over his torso. Far too many of the wounds were rapidly welling blue iridescent blood.

One of the largest pieces had pierced his flesh deeply...impaled him dangerously near his hearts. His right hand was missing below the elbow with torn flesh and jagged bone showing.

Between the multiple shrapnel wounds and his traumatic amputation, the cryogen unit was not able to keep enough ahead of the massive blood loss. His usually amber eyes were a dark, dull brown. They rolled up in his sockets as Kairn finally lost the battle for consciousness.

Looking around with fierce focus, Daria snapped at the medic, "Give me your belt....*Now*, soldier! Concentrate the cryogen unit over his torso—at the large piece of shrapnel near his hearts."

She grabbed the belt the medic hastily offered her. Daria swiftly fashioned a crude, but effective tourniquet above his elbow, buying herself...and Kairn... a few precious moments.

Flicking a steely glance at the hapless medic, Daria ordered in a flat voice, "*Whatever* you do, don't pull that piece of shrapnel out. It's all that's keeping him from bleeding out further. Leave his arm to me!"

Fighting for objectivity, Daria searched with swift thoroughness. Her frustration mounting, she forced herself to slow down. *This is why health care workers don't take care of family...*

Muttering colorful oaths under her breath, Daria nodded grim thanks to Darzik when he lifted Kairn's massive arm into the poor light. A transient movement caught her eye. *Ah...there's the little bugger.*

Despite the tight tourniquet, bright blue blood caught the light as it briskly spurted, pouring Kairn's lifeblood onto the churned up muddy ground with lethal efficiency.

Her hands were slippery with his blood. She clamped her hand over his stump and, desperately fumbling in the poor light, sent up fervent prayers.

Tightening the tourniquet to no avail, Darzik muttered, "Kirov is en route. ETA 6 Earth minutes."

Daria's heart stuttered. *Kairn doesn't have six minutes. So...neither do I. I'm not losing him. I can do this. I have to...because failure is not an option.*

Sending up desperate prayers, Daria dug blindly. Blood pulsed against her fingers. She let out a borderline hysterical laugh as, by feel and a lot of divine guidance, she found the torn artery still pulsating all too briskly. With a hoarse sound of hope and triumph, she pinched the artery closed. Daria gave Darzik a tired but hopeful smile. They both relaxed infinitesimally as the arterial spurting slowed to a slow drip

Closing her eyes in silent prayer, Daria groaned. "*Thank you, God. Please let this be enough. I know you've done a lot, but we still need your help. I can't lose him...*"

Kairn's eyes fluttered. He murmured woozily, "*Molindri...*"

Meeting her eyes, Kairn struggled to focus. He grimaced in pain; holding her gaze, Kairn somehow managed a wan smile—before he drifted back into merciful unconsciousness.

Letting out a ragged breath, Daria exchanged relieved looks with a pale and shaky Darzik. The exhausted XO leaned back slightly. He growled softly, "You are the reason why Kairn is alive. I love him like a brother. So...Thank you...sister."

With a weak smile, Daria nodded a silent thanks. She mentally counted the time remaining on Kirov's ETA. Ruthlessly subduing a surge of anxiety, she didn't move, ignoring the sweat dripping into her eyes; she didn't flinch. Gritting her teeth, she chanted silently to herself. *I can do this.*

Daria bit her lip—tasting blood. *Dear God, please be listening right now. I know we can do this.*

Daria glanced at Kairn's ashen features—willing him to live. Stoically ignoring the brutal cramps starting in her clenched muscles, she kept her fingers locked securely on the key to his survival.

CHAPTER THIRTY-NINE

Daria

She only remembered bits and pieces of the chaotic trip back to the Guardian. The bucking slip and slide of the transport as it tore through the sky at attack speed. The tight vise in her chest when Kairn didn't regain consciousness. The desperate tenuous hold she kept on the slippery torn artery in his stump. The medics rushing around trying to help stabilize the ugly shrapnel protruding from his badly lacerated chest. A grim-faced Kirov accessing a pale (but fiercely determined) Darzik's arm for a direct emergent blood transfusion to a frightfully ashen Kairn.

Daria slumped on a cot next to Kairn's bed; she was almost numb with fatigue. She kept her hand resting over the reassuring steady thrum of his hearts. Daria only distantly registered a general mild ache from where her body had been tossed about. The medics had told her it could have been so much worse.

Anger flickered in her eyes as she thought about the specialized armor she'd been wearing. *Of course, it was his. I am so...angry with him. It...he saved my life, but at what price...*

Things had been dicey for a while. The Luperan Medicos had immersed his battered body in a cryogen tank for a day. From the multiple lacerations sustained by the Ichori's talons, Kairn had developed an insidious, deep muscle infection. Even with the cryogen tank, he required extensive repeated debridements.

His hearts had nearly stopped before he received multiple blood transfusions from his battle brothers. Daria was almost afraid to sleep; she was plagued with the fear that his survival was only a figment of her desperate imagination.

Like a rat on a wheel, her mind ran through the litany of his many injuries. She knew Kairn could have so easily died. Her mind shied away from the thought. Over and over again, she reminded herself. *By some miracle and formidable strength of will, he didn't.*

As minutes...and then hours ticked by without further life-threatening incidents, Daria forced herself to relax in small increments. A tired but luminous smile curved her lips. She kept her fingers stroking tenderly over the reassuringly steady beat of his hearts. Closing her eyes, Daria whispered a poignant thank you to a merciful God—hers... and his.

Daria thought for a moment. She'd lost all track of time. Was this day three...or day four? New jagged scars now showed through his layer of fine fur from the many shrapnel injuries—still angry and raised. The worst one was under her hand...next to his hearts. Her gaze drifted to his well-healing stump. They hadn't found his hand.

Daria shrugged as she absently traced the multitude of scars with gentle fingers. *Scars don't matter. Whatever shape he's in, I'll gladly take him.*

Staving off a yawn, Daria chuckled softly—more than a little punch-drunk with exhaustion. *What's that saying?*

She smiled as the old dusty memory came to her. *Pain heals. Chicks dig scars. It's true!*

Daria lay her head down on Kairn's bed. *At least I do. Your scars prove you're a survivor. I'm ever so grateful that you're here to have them. Thank you for fighting so hard and coming back to me, sweetheart.*

He slept on, heavily medicated. With a soft sigh, Daria finally gave herself permission to sleep, her hand resting on his steadily beating hearts.

A Few Days Later

Darzik and the rest of Kairn's friends came back multiple times a day. She remembered each and every one of them. Their dedication to her Mate spoke volumes.

Breis, the soft-spoken engineer, came by Kairn's bedside every few hours. Breis did not talk much. He just kept vigil with Daria as they both stared silently at Kairn's too still body on the bed—willing him to live.

On one of Breis' many visits, Daria roused herself enough to notice just how worn and pale the young warrior was becoming. Breis had merely smiled and said Kairn was like his brother. Daria noticed idly that Kairn would rally a bit more after these visits.

Surprise lacing his tired hoarse voice, Darzik mentioned that the surviving Ichori from the North Pole was thriving. After initial stiff resistance, he seemed to be bonding with the Ichori bridge crew/resistance members.

Daria's thoughts wandered. It had been a rough day. Kirov, the head Medico, had drawn her quietly aside. He had warned her that Kairn would react poorly.

Amputations were exceedingly rare with their medical technology. Kirov stressed repeatedly and emphatically that a key part of Luperan male identity was his ability to protect his Mate and their family.

Kirov hadn't been able to suppress a pained grimace when he looked at Kairn. "You are a physician on Earth. You know he nearly died—more than once. Many others would have. Amputations are uncommon in Lupera. Most would rather be dead. Lupera is a primarily military society. We are not...open to accepting the neural connections needed for prosthetics to succeed."

Running his hands over his drawn features, Kirov fell quiet for a moment. He continued quietly, "In truth, I do not know if I would be able to make the adjustment...to accept being less than I was. If anyone can, it is Kairn."

Kirov stared at her steadily. He continued with brutal honesty.

"Kairn would do it for you. If you do not think you can accept him as he is now, he is better off without you. Walk away now if you have doubts. Leave him some semblance of peace...before you cause him irreparable harm."

Daria spoke sharply, cold rage edging her voice. "I have no doubts. What's wrong with you? Nothing about Kairn is less! You will never mention that to him. Not in my presence...not ever!"

Daria drew in a long shuddering breath. She snarled fiercely, "Kairn is my Mate. He is alive. His scars are badges of honor. They prove that he is a fighter. That's *all* they mean. Because of that, they're beautiful to me."

Daria drew a shaky breath. "I'm not going anywhere. You're supposed to be his friend. You've fought long and hard to help save him. You know better. You should be ashamed of yourself. If you even attempt to mention that rubbish to him, I will bar you from his bedside permanently."

Kirov sighed. "I am his friend...his brother. By extension, I am yours as well. I wish him no harm. He is one of the best males I have had the privilege to know. His injury is just that...an injury. It does not change what...and who he is. Being Kairn..."

A ghost of a smile crossed his face. "I am sure he will far exceed all of my expectations. I just want you to be prepared. He will not react well to his injury..."

Daria shrugged as she answered curtly, "A normal response. I expect nothing else initially."

Daria stared at Kirov. The anger faded from her...leaving her drained. She managed a wan smile. "That was downright diabolical. Now that I'm a bit calmer, I understand why you did that. I was extremely angry with you, but I know you have only his best interests at heart..."

Daria's smile sweetened as her hands rested on Kairn's chest. She drew in a fortifying breath at the reassuring strong beat of his hearts under her fingers. Her smile deepened as she felt his pulse surge slightly under her lingering touch. She reminded herself. "Hearts.."

Kirov smiled with startling sweetness. "You are good for him. Despite these current circumstances, Kairn is lucky."

Daria shook her head. "I'm the lucky one...and I know it."

Inclining his head deeply, Kirov nodded at her. "I would count you both lucky...sister."

His deep blue eyes were warm with respect before he stalked away.

Daria shook off the memory when she thought she felt Kairn's fingers move. The claws on his metal prosthetic caught the light as his hands moved restlessly. She caught a glint of his amber eyes as they slitted open in slow degrees. Daria closed her eyes for a moment. *I know Kirov meant well...but Dear Lord, I hope Kairn didn't hear any of that shit Kirov was spewing earlier.*

She cradled his prosthetic hand gently in her hands. The alloy was smooth under her touch. She stroked his hand lightly. "Hey, big guy. You had me worried for a while."

Daria met his eyes as he squeezed her fingers. "You scared me. I thought I had lost you."

Kairn smiled sleepily at her. His voice was hoarse, but resonated with aching gentleness. "Daria..."

His gaze sharpening, his smile faded as he frowned suddenly...remembering. "My teams...Did we lose anyone? Any serious injuries?"

Daria caught his hands gently in hers, petted them gently. "No... sweetheart. You're the only one still in the med bay."

Kairn closed his eyes briefly. "Thank the Gods."

He struggled to sit up. Daria rested a hand gently against his hearts. She shook her head regretfully. "You need to get more rest."

Kairn's eyes looked heavy. "Thought I was just dreaming again. Never lose me. Will come back to you...always. *Molindri.* Made promise."

His eyes drifted over his body and caught suddenly...widening as he stared fixedly at his prosthetic. She felt his metal fingers, slightly cooler than his ambient temperature, spasm in hers.

Uncertainty flickered in his eyes as he studied her pale face, worn thin with fatigue and worry. His deep voice was quiet. His voice was distant. "I know I am not the same. I would understand if you wished to renounce..."

His voice deepened as he continued with dogged determination. "Sever our Bond. I will not hold you..."

Kairn's voice trailed off when Daria placed his hand on the bed with exaggerated care. Agitated beyond words, she jumped to her feet— pacing across the room and then back. She leaned close into his face and glared into his startled eyes.

She found her voice. "I would smack you, but you have probably sore spots ALL over. Don't you try to back away from me. After all we've been through. Your crew told me that I was wearing YOUR armor. That if you had been wearing it, you wouldn't have any injuries of note to speak of."

Daria saw Kairn shake his head. He tried to speak. "The risk..."

Her eyes narrowing, Daria held up a finger in silent warning. Kairn raised a surprised brow, but nodded. He stared at her, listening intently. She drew a deep breath, building up steam. Frustrated tears shone in her eyes.

"Don't you DARE think this is guilt. We've only just found each other. I could have LOST you forever...you great wonderful IDIOT! You said you're mine. I've never had someone like that. I'd like to be yours..."

In a frustrated rush, she finished. "Look at me. You're still recovering...and I'm screaming like a fishwife at you!"

Daria stared at him, panting heavily. "And just what does Molindri MEAN?!"

Kairn grasped her hands in both of his. He pulled her down onto his chest. Careful of his still fresh injuries, Daria stilled her instinctive wriggle of protest. "I don't want to hurt you."

Kairn shook his head. "You never cause me pain. Your presence... your touch makes everything better."

He stroked both hands gently...surely...down her back until she calmed. He looked into her eyes as she wriggled until her head nestled over his hearts. He smiled, the specter of uncertainty fading from his glowing eyes.

He nuzzled her hair and took a deep breath, the tension draining from him. He tapped over his hearts. "I value your fire and your strong brave heart. Do not ever change."

His eyes were slowly drifting shut. Kairn fought to remain conscious. "Risk well worth it. My choice. Just want to be worthy of you."

He squeezed her fingers gently with his prosthetic hand. "Never enough Medicos... medics. You saved my life. True that. I understand what you were fighting for...the promise of *us*. I have never been away from you."

Kairn let out a long deep breath. He held her gaze with fierce intensity as he continued. "*Molindri* is Luperan for my soul."

Daria felt any lingering doubts melt away. His words. His truth sank into her. She turned a trusting face into his touch. She felt the rightness of them settle in her bones. *I've never felt so safe. Somehow we just fit. Along the way, he's become my home.*

Her voice was soft and loving. "Rest now sweetheart. I'll be here waiting for you when you wake."

Kairn's eyes began to drift shut. He asked drowsily, a slow smile curving his lips, "Is idiot an affectionate term?"

Daria shook her head tenderly. "Not usually...but you had me worried."

She whispered softly. "I love you, sweetheart."

As his eyes closed, she could almost imagine his quiet voice whisper in answer. Gently. Lovingly. In her mind. *Molindri. My Mate. I love you too.*

CHAPTER FORTY

Kairn

Since he was released from the med bay, they'd been staying in his quarters. Daria was exhausting herself trying to look after him. She would only to drift off after he pulled her close to his hearts.

His thoughts raced...chasing themselves in circles like the feral Cascenti. *Two days ago, I destroyed my comm; I crushed it into dust with my prosthetic when I tried to pick it up. The fear that I could hurt my Daria, albeit inadvertently, haunts my every waking moment...and is turning my dreams into nightmares.*

Since then, Kairn had adopted a new grim routine. Once Daria was asleep, Kairn would painstakingly ease himself off their bed. Kairn tried to find comfort in the knowledge that Daria was finally getting some rest. He would eventually fall into a fitful sleep on the bedside chair.

Every night, Kairn would make his way to medico bay...where Kirov would be awaiting him with unwavering support...punctuated with his usual taciturn—and increasingly colorful—commentary.

Tonight, Kairn knew he was still moving slower than his normal. It had already been more than one Earth week. At least, he was no longer flat on his back in the medico bay. He had just completed another grueling training session with his prosthetic.

Kirov's voice was exasperated. "Answer me this question: Why are we doing this again in the middle of the night? Could it be so your

Mate will not tear into your sorry hide for doing too much? Unlike you, she knows you need your rest to heal properly."

Kairn ignored the pointedly accurate dig. He grunted softly, "Need more practice."

The process of re-training—and improving upon—the shocked neural connections was an exercise in frustration. He tried to dredge up some semblance of patience. Kairn grinned fiercely to himself. He could sense Kirov's frown behind him, constantly worrying that he would push himself too far.

Kairn was driven...but he realized his limits and was doing everything possible to avoid a potentially devastating setback. With a grimace, Kairn forced himself to slow down. He thought about Daria. He could feel his lips curving into a slow smile. *A lifetime with her is a powerful motivator.*

He clenched the fist of his prosthetic hand smoothly. When he relaxed his fist, his hand spasmed. He concentrated. The spasms slowed and largely resolved, but he could see the fine tremor in his outstretched fingers.

Kairn cursed under his breath. His claws extended on his left hand. The prosthetic hand was still. Kairn concentrated and the claws on the prosthetic slowly extended.

Kirov sighed. His voice was soft. "It was a very traumatic injury. You know amputations are rare amongst us. You have to give the nerves time to adapt...And for us to manipulate the connections with the prosthetic."

Kirov rested his hand lightly on Kairn's shoulder. "Call me a hypocrite if you like. Brother, I know you hate hearing this, but...be patient. It will come in time. This prosthetic hand that you hate so much..."

Kirov hesitated briefly. The Medico continued with a sad grimace. "Amputations are so rare and devastating. You are setting a new precedent. You did not know it, but you represent hope to our similarly injured warriors...where before they had none."

Kairn stared nonplussed at Kirov, unable to formulate any response. Kirov added softly, "Not just among our Luperan brethren... but amongst our trusted allies in the Alliance. Perhaps even among humans. Remember that..."

A soft chime broke the tense silence between the old friends. Kairn looked at his comm. Satisfaction radiated from his tone. "He got her. What could have taken so long?"

Kirov's ears perked straight up and flicked with curiosity. They both turned as the door was flung open. Lirinx stalked in, leading an angry, snarling Molly on a short leash.

Hackles up, the shepherd tossed her head with a low growl. Kairn thundered, "What do you mean by doing this?! She is a sentient creature. What is that barbaric contraption you have strapped around her head?"

Lirinx snarled in frustration. His uniform was dusty and wrinkled—and torn. His voice was curt. "*That* is a muzzle."

His voice was rueful and reluctantly amused. "It was quite the sight. That is what happened when she barked and chased staff, both human and Luperan, at the base command. She nearly caught them many times. The humans use the device to keep feral animals from biting."

Molly bared an insolent tooth in reply. Kairn knelt by her side, rubbing her soft ears soothingly. He unbuckled the primitive construct from her head and let it fall to the floor with a sharp metallic clang. Her good nature asserting herself, Molly shook herself—covering Lirinx's abused uniform with yet more fur. The muzzle already forgotten, Molly nosed at his prosthetic curiously. She barked softly, ending with a yip. *Your paw. Hurt much?*

Kairn's hands slowed in surprise. Molly tilted her head and sniffed at his prosthetic. She gave the equivalent of an easy canine shrug. *Your scent is different on this paw. Not change anything. Still YOU.*

Molly nudged his prosthetic with her cold nose. The big shepherd gave him her patented soulful look. Kairn scratched Molly's head obligingly.

His voice was hopeful. "Molly, I pray you are right."

Lirinx brushed at Molly's fine long fur covering his uniform. "Big attitude. Small body."

Kairn smiled in satisfaction. "This is one of the females my Mate needs to see. Where is the other? Emily Garrison. Why is she not here?"

Lirinx's voice was noncommittal. "I spoke with her several times. At considerable length. I told her your Daria really wanted to see her. She could benefit from Emily's support during your convalescence..."

Lirinx's even tone was belied by his pointed words. "Since we have all come to know that you are such a cooperative patient. I suspect the only worse one would be Darzik...since you two are far too much alike."

Lirinx sent Kirov a commiserating look. Kirov grinned slightly. "True that...though Darzik would be even more nightmarish."

Kairn frowned. "Do not deflect. Where is Emily?"

Lirinx grimaced slightly. "She sends her...apologies. She said she knows Daria is strong. That Daria knows that Emily would be with her if she could."

Lirinx held Kairn's glowering gaze. "She said she is not ready to be around so many...of us."

Kairn was silent as he thought. Kirov was furious. "Because we are Luperan...and not human?"

Kairn stated softly, "It is because of our size. We terrify her because we are males of large physical stature."

There was an appalled silence. Kirov snarled angrily, "Who would dare..."

Lirinx added gravely, "She stood a good fifteen Earth feet from us at all times. She took painfully obvious notes of any doors and windows."

Kirov breathed out, the soft sound rife with regret. Into the appalled silence, he stated the obvious. "Access points."

Lirinx pulled an envelope out of his jacket. "Emily gave me this for your Mate."

Kairn held the letter in his prosthetic. His thoughts were a chaotic storm.

As close as they are, Emily is so terrified that she cannot even bring herself to come to see Daria. What did she say? What if Emily tries to poison my Mate against me?

Kairn shuddered in visceral response at the devastating thought. *I cannot keep this from Daria. I have to believe that she knows me. If Daria were to take this negatively, my fears about the prosthetic may not even be an issue anymore.*

Molly bumped Kairn's prosthetic demandingly. *No more talk. Daria's friend is sad and in pain. You cannot help. Daria cannot help. Friend must help herself. Afraid of males. Her words hide this, but I can tell. Time help. Right male...her Mate will heal. You protect...he protect until she is ready.*

With that, Molly slid to the floor in a shameless plea for a belly rub. Kairn smiled, his voice warm with affection. He said thoughtfully, "You are right. Molly, I think you just may be the smartest creature in this room. Just like your human."

They all chuckled when Molly snorted. *How else would we be?*

Kairn laughed, his eyes warm. "That is also more than you have ever said to me before."

Molly got to her feet and shook herself vigorously. *Needed to say, she is good person. Daria loves very much...like a litter mate.*

Kairn got to his feet. "I think Darzik is dreaming of her. He knows she has been injured in the past. It is tearing him apart."

Kairn added quietly, "Lirinx, do whatever is necessary to protect her. She is female; that alone is enough to engender our protection. She is also one of our own."

Lirinx and Kirov nodded in unquestioning agreement. Kairn finished softly, "We take care of Family."

Kairn looked askance at Molly. "I will bring you to Daria as soon as she wakes up."

Affection warmed Kairn's tone as he grinned slowly. "I am guessing you could eat."

Her ears pricking forward, Molly's tail waved furiously. *Now. Eat. Now!*

Her tail stilled as she let out a poignant whine. *See soon? Food can wait. Miss her.*

Kairn's voice was slow and thoughtful. "As do I. Always."

Kairn carefully opened the door. Molly's dancing paws drummed on the floor as she tried to control her excitement.

Kairn turned a smilingly remonstrative look on Molly. She yipped softly and stilled her paws, her body vibrating with eagerness. *Now???*

Kairn stole a look at Daria...lingering over the inviting sight of her still asleep in his bed. "Be gentle."

Molly padded quickly over. She put a massive paw on Daria's shoulder and patted gently. Daria slept peacefully. Molly whined deep in her throat and stuck her cold nose into Daria's hand. Daria's hand started to rub lightly over Molly's ears.

Daria opened her eyes and smiled sleepily at Kairn. "I was wondering where you went sweetheart...I had a dream that Molly was here."

Pushing her head under Daria's hand, Molly woofed indignantly. *Not dream. Right here.*

Daria woke up and stared at a widely grinning Molly. Daria sat straight up and flung her arms around Molly, burying her nose in the dog's thick fur.

Daria stared up at Kairn. "You brought Molly to me. It's the little things..."

Kairn looked back in confusion. *What little things?*

Kairn sat down next to her. "We have heard from Emily. She sends her support and wishes she could be here with you. She gave us this for you."

After a barely discernible hesitation, Kairn handed her a thick envelope. Daria smiled. She recognized Emily's distinctive handwriting.

Holding the letter with careful fingers, Daria laughed gently through her tears. "I understand what she's trying to say. She needs time. You're protecting her. Thank you for doing that for her."

Kairn smiled. *She is not asking me a question. She knows me...and is taking me at my word. To Daria, it was an immutable fact.*

He nodded slowly. *I am humbled by the depth of her trust. My vow...I will always do my best to never disappoint her.*

Daria hugged Molly tight one more time, getting an affectionate lick on her ear in acknowledgement. She let go of Molly who promptly sneezed. The big dog curled up on the floor at the side of the bed, eyes intently locked on her human. Daria grabbed Kairn's hand and tugged him onto the bed. She snuggled trustingly into her spot—close against his hearts. "Just...thank you."

Kairn wrapped his arms around her, monitoring his prosthetic. He was careful to not touch any part of her with it. He sniffed absently at her hair. *Her scent is more familiar to me than my own. I am at a loss as to what to do next.*

Kairn wrestled his mounting frustration and unspoken fear...using it to fuel his determination. *Come what may...whatever the cost to me...I will do what is best for my Daria. She is all that matters...*

CHAPTER FORTY-ONE

Daria

Kairn pulled her closer. Daria eyed him with sudden concern. She thought she felt a hint of desperation leak through his usual calm. *He was even more affectionate than his usual self. Not that I'm complaining...I'm not crazy!*

Kairn dropped a lingering kiss on her lips. "I will leave you to read Emily's letters in privacy. I will check in with my staff."

Daria felt oddly unsettled—as if things between them were suddenly at a crossroads. Kairn was starting to get up when Daria pulled his head down to her. She stared into his startled eyes and saw them flare brightly with hunger. Daria felt herself relax.

She nibbled on his lower lip, soothing the slight sting with gentle teasing flicks of her tongue. "I've missed you."

Daria felt his chest rumble in eager response. Her tongue stole between his lips as he began to pant heavily. His tongue rubbed slowly against hers and followed her tongue's teasing touches back into her mouth. He explored her lips and mouth with spine-tingling detail.

She shifted onto his lap, feeling his cock leap eagerly against her. Daria slowly pulled her lips away.

Kairn groaned, his eyes glowing. She dipped her head and traced the line of his jaw. His head dropped back as he growled. She dropped light kisses along his strong neck as he turned into her caresses.

She lingered over the thick tendon as his pulse raced against her lips. Daria smiled at his open response to her slightest touch as a tight knot in her chest unraveled.

Daria's voice was husky as her breathing picked up. "I'm going to give you some incentive to finish up that meeting..."

She kissed his burning skin. She noted that he had a fine sheen of perspiration beading on his skin. Daria took her time and licked over his pulse. She argued with herself. *I shouldn't do it. I'm not a hormone crazed teenager.*

The salt and spice taste of his sweat slammed into her. *I'm a woman crazy in love with this male...my male. I want...need to show him...and everyone.*

Daria opened her mouth. She sucked lightly at first and then gradually harder—lingering over his suddenly hammering pulse. His hips bucked hungrily against her, his cock sliding against her belly.

Daria lifted her head slowly. With deep satisfaction, she traced a gentle finger over the bright blue bruise she'd left. Meeting his enthralled gaze, Daria felt a irrational surge of pride. *Hmmm...that'll leave a mark for a while.*

Daria held Kairn's half-slitted eyes. She blinked at the bright light gold color. His lungs were working like a bellows. His cock stretched midway up his hard belly, pulsing with each beat of his hearts.

Daria stared at him. "Come back to me."

Kairn stared back at her. He reached a hand up to his bruised throat. His smile was primitive, feral, and uncompromisingly hungry. His fingers explored the vivid mark with reverence.

Kairn slammed a fist to his hearts and bowed formally to her. His voice was a rumbling growl. His incandescent gaze lingered on her.

"My hearts-felt thanks for this honor, *Molindri*."

Before he went out the door, Kairn turned. His fingers reached up, unconsciously tracing slowly over the monster hickey she'd given him. "I hope the letters find Emily well. I will be back as soon as I can."

His cock still made an impressive tent in his trousers. Kairn snagged a long uniform jacket and left it hanging open, a token attempt at camouflaging his erection.

Daria felt a pang of guilt about his very obvious condition. She asked ruefully, "That was a tease. Too much?"

Kairn turned with a look of stark disbelief and pride. His voice was poignantly tender and hungry. "Never too much. You claim me as yours...and I will wear both with pride. Anyone who sees me will have pangs of envy at my fierce Mate."

CHAPTER FORTY-TWO

Kairn

Kairn faced each obstacle with grim determination. He utilized any lingering pain as a spur to his mobility. He quickly learned the more he moved, the less he hurt.

Daria had taken indefinite leave to help him with his recovery. At first, Kairn could not control the strength of his prosthetic arm. She had encouraged him when he shattered serving dishes, all manner of glassware, and durable comms. One after the other.

As more time passed, his fears for Daria's safety escalated. Every night, while Daria slept, he spent grueling hours in the medical lab.

Under Kirov's worried eyes, Kairn shattered countless instruments as he learned to gauge his strength appropriately. Kairn pushed himself relentlessly—until Kirov finally nodded approvingly. Kairn now had adequate control of his prosthetic.

Kairn was conflicted. Daria was his world. He wanted only the best for her. If they shared pleasure, he did not know what would happen if...*when* he inevitably lost control. *I am afraid to touch her as I truly want...need to...*

Daria spent as much time with him as he would allow. The memory of her most recent farewell was fresh in his mind, sending hot blood surging into his already throbbing erection.

He had argued bitterly with himself over giving Daria the letter. He trusted that his Mate knew him well, but he worried that the contents of Emily's letter would cause her pain.

Her lush curvy body stirred him, but...even more importantly...just her warm presence at his side made his hearts leap. He treasured her for so many things. He missed her gentle humor, open affection, quick observant mind...the way she would touch him—even in casual passing—with aching tenderness.

When she was not with him, his arms and hearts felt empty. Kairn mourned her absence much more than he missed his arm.

Remembering the way his XO looked at Emily, Kairn smiled. With the exception of Darzik, Kairn had approached each of his oldest friends. One after another, he tracked them down—asking them to consider courting his Mate. Kairn corrected himself sharply. *My intended Mate.*

He ground his teeth and felt his canines lengthen as he felt everything in him revolt viciously at the very thought.

Kairn reminded himself repeatedly...*It would keep her safe.*

He forced himself to continue. *I have to find her a Mate who will not hurt her because he lost control.*

As per his request, his friends were waiting for him in his quarters. They were all pacing the floor restlessly. They stopped when he walked in, eyeing him warily. Kairn tried to voice his request but found he could not bring himself to speak the words.

Darzik spoke first. He pointed at the large unmistakable bruise proudly adorning Kairn's neck. "To get that..."

Darzik shook his head decisively. "It is obvious that your Mate has no fear of you and trusts you. We have all seen that you are trying to distance yourself from Daria. You are not subtle."

Darzik growled at him. "You need to stop tormenting yourself. And Daria."

Kirov muttered. "And us..."

Darzik nodded with a loud snort. "Kirov told us of your initial problems with your prosthetic. You are one of my oldest and closest friends. I will never lie to you. It will destroy you both if you continue this madness. Do not throw this away. Your Daria is a gift. Treasure her as we all know you will. You would never hurt her. You are not capable of it."

Kairn ground out, "Of course not. Not intentionally...but I lose control when we share pleasure."

Kairn raised a hand in unconscious pride to his throbbing neck. "This was a close thing. I do not know how much longer I can keep myself from touching her. No matter what I want, I will not put Daria at risk."

Kirov was calm. "Hear us out. You are Family. We want the best for you...and that is Daria."

Kirov met his gaze squarely. "I can assure you. You represent hope to our veterans. From a medical standpoint, you have control with your prosthetic. More than I dared even hope was possible. Do not use that as your excuse when you choose not to be with her. You are reacting to an unreasonable fear. You will not...CANNOT hurt her. Your instincts will not allow it."

Lirinx spoke at last. "I watched her. She was at your bedside whenever any of us came by."

There were silent nods of agreement all around. Lirinx continued in his even tone, "She wore herself out. She would not leave...not to eat...not to sleep."

Lirinx added succinctly, "Daria does not see us. To her, you are her Mate. Just as she is yours. Deny it all you want. It does not change what you know is truth."

Lirinx tapped his hand over his hearts. "It does not change what is written irrevocably into your hearts. You have to know that we all envy what you have found with her. To have a Mate...it is an unattainable dream for most of us."

Breis was shy and reticent, especially for a Luperan. He chose his words carefully. "In your Mate, you have found what we all hope for.

Your Daria is very special. What is it doing to you...to offer the greatest gift you will ever have to males who will not treat her a fraction as well as you would?"

Breis said more softly, "Just imagine. What if one of us tried to accept Daria? There is no forcing a Mate. My instincts do not engage around her. I cannot...will not make her my world. You nearly died. If I had injuries like yours, I would not choose to live for Daria...to fight so hard to be with her. She is not my Mate. Not Darzik's...or Kirov's... or Lirinx's. She is yours! You are the single best male for her. That you even worry about the impossibility that you would hurt her...only proves anew the depth of your commitment and devotion."

Kairn felt his hearts stutter and begin to race. *I need to find Daria. My friends speak the truth.*

With a wistful smile, Breis shook his head. "That is proof that you are her true Mate. She is the single most important thing in your life. You cannot hurt her. In your hearts, you know this to be true."

Looking into their haggard faces, Kairn realized this ordeal had taken its toll on them all. "You are true friends and brothers. I have not been thinking straight. I have been blind. You have my sincere apologies for even suggesting this travesty—as well as my permission to take your frustrations out in the sparring arena when next we meet."

Their faces relaxed in relief. Breis rubbed his jaw. "I am glad you are finally thinking clearly. You had us well and truly concerned. I...we had never seen you behave like this."

Kairn looked at them with a wicked grin. "Erratically? Irrationally? Utterly devoted to my Mate?"

Kairn laughed with sudden absolute certainty. "Your time will come, my old friends. May you enjoy every intoxicating minute of it. I will be there for you as you have been for me. I will take my leave of you now."

Kairn gripped each of their arms in hearts-felt gratitude before he left the room. Kairn clapped Breis on his shoulders. The young engineer still appeared paler than normal. "I know well what you did for me, Breis."

Kairn eyed him critically. "You push yourself too far."

Breis grinned. "You make a poor patient. We had to get you back on your feet before you drove your Mate—and us—stark raving mad."

Breis tilted his head as he added ruefully, "It was a close thing."

Kairn shook his head. "Enough said. My hearts-felt thanks, brother. I must find Daria to explain my brief insanity."

Darzik laughed softly and called after him, "She already knows. She said to ignore your...how did she put it? Ah...your delusions of martyrdom. Your Mate has an interesting way with words. She said she would take you however she could get you. She said she thanks her lucky stars that you found her."

Darzik look at Kairn questioningly. "I did not know there were fortunate stars."

Pausing to look back over his shoulder, Kairn tilted a quizzical ear. "The odd nonsensical intricacies of English slang. You become accustomed to it. It has become an enjoyable game we share together. It can be quite amusing."

Kairn fell silent for a moment. *And arousing.*

A broad anticipatory smile dawned on Kairn's lips, his eyes beginning to glow as he thought about his wonderful Mate. "I know full well that I am the lucky one."

His friends all laughed. Darzik grinned at him. "By the way, we know we are Family. She says she is adopting the lot of us. She has told us we are like the brothers she never had. You have chosen well."

Darzik's grin softened into a wistful smile. "Remember, brother. Bonding your mate until her lips are swollen...when she proudly shows off the marks of your shared pleasure...this is not injury in your Mate's or our minds! Go claim your Mate!"

CHAPTER FORTY-THREE

Daria

Daria had always suspected it, but now she had irrefutable proof. Kairn made a truly HORRIBLE patient. He hated pain medications. He got up early and stayed up late pushing all the reasonable limits of his rehab. He hounded his prosthetic designers. He DID heal rapidly.

He used his prosthetic until it seemed a part of him. Not unexpectedly, he had some early minor mishaps with control. Kairn had badgered a beleaguered Kirov repetitively. The irate Medico manipulated the delicate neural interface connections with precision. Kairn now had the same...or better sensation and control in his prosthetic as he did in his original hand.

She shook her head and sighed. Kairn had always pointedly sought her out. He had made time in his hectic schedule for her.

Daria was lost in thought. She knew Kairn was warm and attentive. When he was with her, he was unstintingly and openly affectionate. Generous in his praise.

Kairn stared at her hungrily with his eyes glowing molten gold. Considerate and fiercely protective. He was unfailingly courteous, but otherwise blind to other women. He proudly introduced her to his close friends and crew. He was rather blatantly possessive (so was she). She frowned...*Though he wasn't nearly as much recently.*

Her frown deepened as she reflected on the past few weeks. Of late, he was always on the bridge. In engineering. Running drills with security. Sparring in the gym with Darzik.

In short, he had made her feel like she was the center of his world. That had not changed, but he was running himself ragged. His face was etched with lines of fatigue when he finally came to their bed. Daria could not help the sense that his hectic schedule was deliberate.

Every day, she was waking to half remembered dreams of him—her body restless and flushed with lingering echoes of intense pleasure.

Daria shook her head. She needed something to clear her head. She smiled as she remembered Emily's letter.

She retrieved it and carefully opened it. She smiled at Emily's obsessively neat handwriting.

Daria,

I hope this finds everything OK with you. I'm sorry, but I'm not ready to talk about this face to face.

I was attacked when I was on Spring Break my last year of nursing school. I was green as grass. I was roofied by a stranger. I didn't know what he looked like or his name...not then. I woke up sore and with bruises in places I don't like to remember. To state the obvious, it was apparently not an enjoyable or gentle experience. I consider myself lucky that I can't recall any details. He was my first. And last.

He was found. The trial dragged on forever. It's a dark time in my life I choose not to dwell on. I changed my name. Who I used to be doesn't matter. That foolish child is dead and buried.

I'm far better than I used to be, but I'm still not comfortable being around men...particularly large men. I get bad flashbacks. I talk a big game to keep guys away from me. Cuz...you know... they've got to live up to all the imaginary guys before them.

I'm very cynical...I know. But...What has given me hope is how you are with Kairn. And he is with you. I wish you could see how he looks at you. It's like you're Wonder Woman and the one -that - got- away girl next door. All rolled up in warm butter, cinnamon, and fresh sugar.

Seriously, your male (cuz that's what he is) always looks like he could eat you alive. His first touch whenever he sees you is like he's about to touch the Holy Grail. Downright reverent. And then becomes all alpha male possessive and protective. Watching y'all gives me chills...the good kind. Let me tell you girl...I'm thinking you'd die a happy woman.

I know you haven't had a lot to do with guys before. And I'm a fine one to be handing out advice on your love life...but I'm going to anyway.

Go with your instincts. Trust your heart. You've got a good one. And so does he. I watch people a lot. From what I've seen, he already considers himself yours...and yours alone. That fine boy (I can look, but I won't touch!) is WAY off the market.

Take a chance. Don't be like me. Don't let fear of the what-might-happens rule you. Have faith and take that next great step into the rest of your amazing life. I'm thinking Kairn will be there to catch you and be with you every step of the way.

Much love,

Emily

P.S. Say hello to your male and tell him thanks for the security detail. They weren't that subtle. I expect an invite to the wedding. Or whatever the hell y'all will call it. I'll be there with bells on.

A teardrop landed on the shaking leaves of paper in her hand. Daria wiped at the tears trickling down her face. She could hear Emily's sarcastic voice in her ear as she read her letter. *It sounds just like her. The smart ass!*

Daria sniffled. Emily was in so much pain but managed to reach out to help her with issues with Kairn.

She had to think this through logically. She knew she was quickly becoming irritable with frustrated desire...because when she did see him, she was usually the initiator of their abbreviated kisses. His touch was tender, but brief and...never with his prosthetic hand.

Daria shook her head in pained understanding. *Duh. Really? He surely doesn't think it makes any difference to me...Males! It didn't matter what species.*

A wicked smile slowly curved her lips.

CHAPTER FORTY-FOUR

Kairn

Kairn paced over the lush grass, tail flicking in irritation. He was meeting Daria here, but she had been curiously evasive on the reasons why. No one else was there. The solarium was cool and quiet, with the vibrant scent of living plants.

Large targets were set back in the trees for friendly competitions to test the balance of precision throwing blades. Daria had teased him and called it "darts on steroids." Kairn smiled at the memory. *I miss her.*

His ruff prickled. He was dreaming of her, reliving the vivid memories of what they shared in exquisite arousing detail. Every night fed his growing need for her. He was ready to explode with the instinctive drive to show her what she meant to him. Kairn felt hunger hammer at the limits of his control.

He stared at his prosthetic. Kairn flexed his fingers slowly, drawing two blades from his boots. He rotated both hands through intricate maneuvers with the weapons. He examined their results, darts vibrating deep and true in the targets. The accuracy and depths the darts sank into the targets were nearly perfectly symmetrical and reproducible on both hands.

A tender smile crossed his lips. He would always call them darts now because of Daria. *I know she would laugh at the sound of that. Darts for Daria.*

He felt his shoulders relax a fraction. If anything, his control was better with the prosthetic arm than his native one.

He heard the door open. Kairn turned as Daria slipped in. He lifted a brow as she made sure to lock it securely behind her. Daria smiled sweetly at him as he stood silently watching her. She walked slowly over to him, her bare feet sinking into the thick grass.

He stared fixedly at her—and wondered when she took her shoes off. Kairn smiled slightly to himself. *I even find her little toes—shockingly absent of any protective armament—adorable and strangely intimate.*

Kairn fought to form a sentence. "Is Emily well?"

Silently berating himself, he stifled a groan. *That perhaps may not have been my best choice of questions.*

Kairn grumbled a warning as she strode right up and snuggled into his chest. She rested her hand on his right arm. She smiled at him as she slid his sleeve up to where the prosthetic attached seamlessly.

Daria trailed her fingers over his hot skin, petting absently at the flexing muscles. Daria looked up and met his guarded gaze. "Emily is doing OK for now. With time, she'll do even better. Emily says hello and thanks you for the security. Her letter just said what I already knew."

She rubbed her head over his hearts. He heard her inhale deeply and felt a subtle tension ebb from her. Rippling with sudden heat, his voice was gravelly and incredulous. "Did you just sniff me?"

Daria laughed softly. She grazed her nose through his fur, taking a long deep breath. "I know it's kinda your thing, but I absolutely did."

Making no effort to disguise her pleasure, she sniffed again. "Mm-mmm...you smell soooo good. I missed you."

His large frame shivered with his inevitable response to her. He tried to suppress his growl. "Just what are you about?"

She tilted her head up and met his burning eyes. Her voice was soft and sure. Intimate. "Finally listening to my heart. Faith. Trust. Love. High time to claim what is mine."

He stared at her. "You deserve..."

She nipped him sharply over his hearts. "You shouldn't finish that sentence."

His hands lifted to her shoulders as he tried to push her gently back. With a soft growl Daria burrowed deeper against his chest. She slipped her arms around his waist with a soft sigh. Daria stared intently into his startled wondering gaze. With sweet certainty, she declared, "Stop pushing your friends at me."

Daria didn't bother to hide a shudder of distaste. "It's creepy. In case you didn't know, it's nearly incest at this point. They're like Family to me. The very idea...it would be like kissing my brother...if I had one."

She cupped his jaw in her hand, stroking over his skin. "Trust me to know what...and *who* I want...who I *need*..."

Determination in her gaze, she continued. "You've always fought for us. Now it's my turn."

Her eyes soft and warm, Daria caught her lower lip in her teeth. "Let me show you."

Her voice caught—grew husky. "I *need* to show you."

His skin burned as if with fever. He could deny her nothing. They dropped to the soft floor as her exploring fingers made a slow tease of his uniform fastenings. His clothes fell off his massive frame. He made quick work of hers. Their bodies dropped to the soft grass, melding together.

CHAPTER FORTY-FIVE

Daria

D aria met his eyes as she eased over his restless body. She settled her hips over his muscled belly. His body surged against her with rampant hunger. A hard bar with a fine coat of silken velvet stroked over her lower belly in a burning caress. She shifted her body. Holding his gaze, she moved in slow firm strokes over his cock, tantalizing them both. His chest rumbled in a hungry growl.

She leaned over him and felt heat pulse in her core. He panted as she drew in his warm breath, savoring his wild flavor. A soft moan escaped her. His canines lengthened as he slowly drew in her breath... and her scent. Over and over, they shared their breath. She felt hot moisture slick between her legs as his hips lifted hard against her.

Daria brushed her lips over his jaw, teased over his lips. She felt his growl rumble through her. Her tongue traced his sharp teeth. With a small smile, she traced a careful path along his fang.

As her eyes met his, she slid her tongue against the tip with a small deliberate scrape—until she wept small droplets of blood. Her tongue slipped into his mouth and slid against his. He groaned at the rich taste of her blood. His tongue thrust deep into her mouth. His arms wrapped snug around her, pulling her even closer.

Gasping, she broke away. She smiled and drew his right arm up to her face. "Can you feel this?"

She explored his prosthetic with gentle fingers. Pressed a firm kiss to his wide palm. Licked his skin slowly. "And this?"

A continuous growl rumbled from his chest. A fine tremor shook his right hand...his prosthetic as she lifted it slowly. "Right now, it's just another part of you."

Daria traced the lines of his sleek prosthetic...of his hand with aching tenderness. "THIS brought you back to me. I give thanks every day for this prosthetic that you hate so much. You are alive. I will take you however I can get you."

With a broken laugh, Daria pressed her lips to the back of his hand...his prosthetic hand...in a tender kiss. "I know this has been hard. I'm proud of you. Thank you for coming back to me, sweetheart."

Kairn stared at her, his eyes soft with wonder. His voice was raw. "I can feel your touch on my hand. On the prosthetic."

He looked at her, his gaze stark with pain. "My control was lacking. I still fear I will hurt you. I would rather not ever touch you again than take the chance of injuring you."

Daria racked her hunger-drunk brain. *Everything hinges on what I say next. Wonderful, trustworthy overprotective Kairn. It's my turn to fight for us.*

She chose her words with care. "Amputations are sadly more common on earth. You had some minor problems when you first came out of sedation. It's normal to have an adjustment period."

She rested her shaking hand against his pounding hearts. "My Mate..."

Daria felt him shiver at her words. "Sweetheart, you have exquisite control. I love that you even think to worry about this. I know you."

Daria looked into his eyes. She spoke her unvarnished truth. "I trust you. You will never hurt me with this arm. It's part of you...I dream about touching you. I want you to touch me. You will hurt me if you deny us...what we are...what we will *always* be to each other."

She met his eyes and saw understanding and—finally—hard-won exquisite acceptance dawn in his eyes. Holding his gaze, she nestled closer against his chest, her hard nipples tickling his skin.

His pupils dilated wildly and he pounced.

CHAPTER FORTY-SIX

Kairn

Kairn could hardly put his thoughts to speech. His body burned with need. Her scent. Her taste. The trusting look in her eyes. He found her intoxicating. He remembered a line in the Western human joining ceremony. *With my body, I thee worship. Truer words had never been spoken.*

She lay beneath him, her body shivering with anticipation. His hand flexed slowly on her breast. His fingers traced over her. He retracted his claws, then teased her nipple with slowly tightening circles.

Kairn rested his hand over her heart. He managed a monosyllable and ground out "Mine."

He slammed his other hand over his hearts and growled. "My vow. Yours. Always."

She stared back at him and breathed out with a tremulous smile. "Always."

His eyes made promises. He saw their future in her face. After long seconds, he broke away. "I cannot wait any longer, *Molindri.*"

His lips made slow sweeps over her, learning her body. The arch of her neck. The sweet tempting juncture between neck and shoulder. His hands pulled her tight into the protective shelter of his body. He traced a path down her chest and counted each individual delicate rib; using exquisite care, he mapped each one with slow laps of his tongue.

Daria moved restlessly, her hands pulling at him. "Kairn. Please hurry. I...ache."

Kairn wound his tail gently around her thigh and opened her fully to him. His hips settled firmly in the cradle of her body. "Slow is better."

Kairn's eyes danced with heated playfulness. He smiled into her eyes. "Foreplay..."

His cock slid slow and sure between her slick hot lips. His voice was a barely audible growl. "So...wet. Hot. Soft."

They both groaned. He thrust helplessly for long moments, learning her heat.

He took a deep breath. He cradled her breast in his massive hand, learning the soft smooth skin. He nuzzled the taut nipple. With a soft groan, he licked slowly over and around it. Kairn suckled gently, Daria's soft cries guiding him.

He suckled hard, drawing her breast into his mouth. He was rewarded by a soft scream. He breathed on her engorged red nipple and bit gently. Her body arched soundlessly. He felt a gentle rain of her warm thick liquid kiss the head of his cock—tracking slow and rich along his shaft.

He lifted his body and reached a gentle fingertip to collect the gift of her creamy desire where it adorned his cock, mixing with his seed slowly beading on the head. Kairn lapped it off his fingertip...and sucked his finger clean. His cock jerked heavily and increased again in girth as he savored the intoxicating taste of their shared pleasure.

With a slow smile, Kairn then reached for her neglected breast with single minded intensity.

CHAPTER FORTY-SEVEN

Daria

Daria stirred groggily, her body awash with pleasure. Stroking his hands soothingly from her shoulders to her knees, Kairn leaned over her with a slow hungry smile.

His cock nudged insistently against her belly. Daria stared at him with a delicious surge of rekindling hunger. She remembered well the hot slide of him in her hands—the long thick shaft with blue veins showing through his grey skin.

He smoothed out to a large purple red head. His shaft throbbed eagerly. Daria watched as light blue pearly fluid welled at the slit and slid slowly along his shaft.

His large balls were lightly furred and drawn tight to his body. The ache between her legs pulsed as she remembered the tangible trust between them and the incredible pleasure they had shared together.

Daria groaned softly and tugged at his shoulders. "Come to me."

Kairn leaned back, his eyes intent. "I am not done yet, *Molindri*."

He sank slowly to his haunches. Daria stared wide-eyed and tried to close her legs. Kairn reached up and slid a tender hand along her jawline. Their eyes met as Kairn settled between her legs. He smiled before he eased her legs over his shoulders. "Trust me."

His eyes shifted down and he stared for long moments. He leaned forward and took a deep breath. "Your scent...you smell so good."

Daria felt more moisture well hot and slick from her core. Kairn looked up briefly. "What do we call this?"

Daria felt a hot blush all over, her feet twitching. "Vagi...no. Pussy."

Kairn managed a brief smile at her before his gaze turned back. Daria couldn't move as Kairn took another slow deep breath. His hands slid between her thighs. He carefully retracted the claws on his long thick fingers.

She panted as he held up his prosthetic. His eyes were soft. She could feel the smoother...cooler metal of his prosthetic fingers as he ran them down her slit and carefully pulled her lips apart. "Pretty, Molindri. You are so pink and pretty here."

Daria's fingers locked in his long hair on his head, tugging urgently. His head lowered; his warm breath teased her aching core.

Kairn's eyes slitted to half-mast as his long blue tongue lapped at the moisture slowly welling out of her pussy. A deep growl vibrated his tongue and her hips bucked wildly. He wrapped his hands around her hips, lifting her to his lips.

CHAPTER FORTY-EIGHT

Kairn

Kairn mapped her soft folds slowly with his tongue. He watched her responses. First light touches: elicited a gasp. Firm strokes: provoked a breathless sigh.

Kairn bathed the sensitive nub at her apex with slowly tightening circles and a slow gentle bite...A short scream. Sharp pain behind his ears where she pulled out clumps of fur. He growled softly. *Ah. She likes this. Noted.*

Kairn slid his tongue down from her nub. He sucked on her sensitive outer lips, then kissed them gently. Their eyes met as he slid his tongue into the narrow spasming channel of her pussy. Kairn closed his eyes in pleasure. *Her trust. Dear Gods, her taste. I will never get enough of her.*

His tongue thrust—slow and deep. He felt her slick walls tighten around him. Again, and again. Daria arched her hips in hungry demand. Kairn lifted his head reluctantly and leaned back. He licked his lips, his eyes slitting nearly closed at her taste.

Daria's body shifted restlessly. Karin traced a silver metal finger along the edges of her pulsing slit. He looked up at Daria as he slid his finger into her writhing body. His cock throbbed. She was hot. Soft. Tight and wet.

Daria caught her swollen lip in her teeth and moaned, hips twisting toward him. She breathed "Now!"

Kairn drew his finger out, her body twisting and clenching tight around it—then deliberately pumped it in again. His finger slid slow and deep to his last knuckle. In and out.

He added another thick finger and thrust deeply as he explored her sleek spasming walls. He coaxed rich moisture from her until it pooled warmly in his palm.

The air was filled with his deep groans, her soft sighs, and the wet sound of his hungry fingers readying her body. Kairn's control snapped.

He pulled his fingers from her. Her voice trailed off. "Nooooo! What are..."

She stared as he finished licking her glistening wetness from his fingers. Kairn smiled. "You taste so good."

He moved over her and brought her close to his chest. He slid her open legs even wider and rolled over on his back. He joined their lips in a hard kiss, tongues slowly twining. He knew she could taste herself in his kiss as he leaned back. His cock brushed hot and wet high against her belly.

He slanted her a smile of singular tenderness edged with shared hunger. He brought her fingers to rest on his chest. She felt his hearts pause and align to match her pulse. He groaned. "Yours. Together."

Together

Daria sat up and slid up his belly. He growled as warm silkiness dripping from her pussy coated his skin. Her hips arched as the head of his cock parted her lips with a soft wet sound. The mouth of her pussy clenched hungrily and his large head slid in slowly past her small entrance.

She hummed. Gasped softly. Her hips hovered. "Oh...Feels tight."

His long finger swept through her wetness and circled her nub. He flicked lightly with his fingertip. With careful control, he extended the merest hint of his claw—and tapped it gently. He murmured. "What do we call this?"

For a moment, her mind blanked. *What had he asked?*

Through the delicious clouds of sensation, Daria gathered her scattered thoughts. "My...uh... clit."

His amber eyes were bright gold. He smiled fiercely. His voice was a guttural growl. He repeated the evocative word succinctly. "Your clit."

Kairn leaned over to nuzzle the inside of her thigh. Flashing her a hungry smile, he pressed a lingering skin to her sensitive skin. "Nerve center of pleasure for you."

Kairn stared into her eyes, holding her gaze—before he flicked it again. Her vision turned white for long blissful seconds. Kairn caught her hands as she fell forward. He slid his fingers through the rich warm moisture flowing freely from her body.

Kairn smiled hungrily into her wide stunned eyes. They both watched as he spread her wetness over his shaft. He ran tender fingers along her lips stretched tightly around him. He eased a finger alongside his shaft and gathered the silky seed welling from his slit, gently stretching her.

Daria slowly sank down onto his lap. His cock slid in with a delicious burn until his wide base wedged against her folds. His tail wrapped around her upper leg, the fine short fur tickling her inner thigh.

His hands moved to her sides. Kairn grasped her hips tightly, his fingers opening and closing. She wanted to chase the fine droplets of sweat that had broken out on his chest and follow the grooves down his muscled belly. Her hips flexed in involuntary response.

Kairn was rigidly still beneath her, his only sounds were ragged breathing and a continuous low snarl. He ground out. "Any pain, my Daria?"

Daria moved her hips in a lazy circle, delicious pressure gradually building. She answered dreamily. "Hmmm...No. Good. You feel so good."

Her hips lifted up and down. Slow up and fast down. And again. She sighed...her voice breaking. "I need more, sweetheart. Move. Please."

Kairn's hip thrust up once, twice. He stopped and ground out. "Tell me if this is too much."

Her fingers twisted into his hair, tugging restlessly. "Noooo...Don't stop!"

His ears rotated alertly as his hips flexed. He memorized what she liked. Slow and Deep. Her cries were soft. Hard and deep so he could hear the slick welcoming sound of their heated flesh coming together as he thrust in and out—pulled a scream. Her baby claws raked down his back; they left tiny trails of intoxicating fire in their dainty wake. Kairn fought to commit the exquisite details to memory. Her walls fluttered tight and wet around him in silent irresistible demand.

His control splintered. Kairn pulled Daria into the shelter of his chest. His hearts raced as he pulled his cock out, glistening with both their pleasure. He met her heavy-lidded gaze. Her hands pulling at him, Daria nodded fiercely...and Kairn slammed home.

Groans rumbled deep in his throat. Kairn's body worked tirelessly under her. His skin beaded with sweat as his hips pumped in a hard driving rhythm, hammering home...pistoning until her walls spasmed—tightening into a sleek hot vise around him.

Daria stared down at him. Her half-closed eyes were soft with tenderness. They hazed as pleasure splintered through her. Her body clenched, her hot thick moisture bathing his cock.

Daria screamed softly. She pressed her open mouth against his chest in an instinctive seeking motion. Daria bit his chest over his hearts; her blunt teeth broke his skin and drew small droplets of blood. At his Mate's bite, Kairn's body convulsed. He roared with pleasure, thrusting wildly as he came inside her with hot fountains of seed.

She collapsed bonelessly on his heaving chest. He stroked her back, scratching lightly with his claws. Kairn lifted her off gently, dropping soft kisses on her nose and upturned lips. He pulled her close into the shelter of his body and sniffed deeply of her tousled hair. *She smells like home.*

She woke briefly with a sleepy grumble which he solved with long sweet minutes of gentle back scratching. A smile curved his lips as she cuddled closer and rested her head over his hearts.

The soft sounds of her peaceful breathing sent gentle waves of contentment through him. Kairn smiled as he stared dreamily at the canopy of leaves sheltering them. *A good start on learning what pleases my Mate.*

CHAPTER FORTY-NINE

Daria

Daria opened her eyes in the dim light. A thick blue vine draped over the mantle, scattered with young leaves in widely varying shades of rich blues. It was just beginning to bud. A deep breath brought a light herbal scent to tickle her nose. Sometime during the long incredible night, Kairn had brought her to his room.

She stretched lazily, feeling a satisfied burn in her replete muscles. His hard body curved around her; the fine dusting of silky soft fur on his chest tickled her spine in a subtle caress Kairn's hard cock flexed and pressed against her ass. Daria rubbed her hips against him. She moved to turn over but was swept back.

Her legs parted in a sleepy response. She felt a warm liquid pooling between her legs. She looked down and watched a slow trickle of thick creamy fluid well up from the swollen lips of her deliciously aching pussy.

It was a telling shade of very light blue. As she stared at the evidence of their pleasure, her nipples stiffened. Desire stirred again deep inside. Wet and hot. She felt so empty.

His warm spiced breath washed over her nape and she felt his jaw tuck her head closer. He rumbled sleepily, "You feel good. It is early still. Do not get up yet."

She pushed her hips back in hungry demand. Kairn woke fully with an appreciative growl. His large hands held her searching hips in place.

She tried to move, her hips twisting. His voice was gruff, tender, deepening with hunger. He grunted. "It is too soon. I do not want to hurt you."

Daria cried out softly in welcome when Kairn slid a slow hand between her parted thighs. He delved into her soft swollen folds. Kairn explored her gently in slow tight circles.

Daria arched her hips. She heard the slick sound as his long thick finger parted her, sliding home. Deep and slow. Daria felt a slight twinge.

His voice breathed softly in her ear. "Too tender."

Daria tugged at him. Her voice was husky from screaming. "In a very good way. *Not* sore."

Kairn smiled tenderly at her. "I will take care of you, *Molindri*. Always."

He was panting heavily as he kissed her deeply, hot and hungry. Their tongues twined together and released. And again.

His fingers spread her creamy moisture over her. They danced over her sensitive clit as Daria writhed in his arms. He drummed lightly, then drove her up with escalating tempo and pressure. Kairn added another finger and slid deep, brushed against that sensitive spot inside her. In and out. He pushed her over the edge with a firm pinch to her throbbing clit. Her pussy clenched in rhythmic spasms as her body tightened in powerful release.

Kairn growled continuously in his chest. A long deep howl tore from his throat. Daria felt his cock throb in heavy long pulses. Hot silky liquid looped over her hips and back as his seed marked her as his.

Daria felt his chest heaving rapidly still against her back. She felt him nuzzle her hair, her neck. She heard Kairn sniff deeply—then felt him let out a soft contented sigh. Nearly boneless, Daria lay there idly running her hand slowly along his arm. She didn't notice his prosthetic.

Kairn leaned back and slowly pulled his fingers out of her. The wet hungry sound made them both shiver with pleasure. She felt her pussy cling tightly to him, vibrating with small aftershocks. Daria turned to look at him, questions in her eyes. She took care not to roll onto her back.

Kairn touched her back with tender hungry hands. Daria felt his long finger dip into a puddle of his silky seed—still warm from his body. He made to sit up. Though his eyes were carefully guarded, his voice was tender. "I will bring something to clean this up."

Daria's heart broke slightly at his attempt to hide his pain and need from her. Her voice was very gentle. Soft. Certain. "Don't. Please."

He stared at her. He was silent, but hope rose in his eyes. "*Molindri*..."

Daria looked steadily at him. She willed him to see her understanding and eager acceptance. Her blatant need. She spoke, breathtaking in her candor.

"With what we share, I would hate it if you washed my pleasure off you..."

Her eyes drifted down the long length of his body—lingered on his still hard cock gleaming wetly with the evidence of their shared pleasure. She continued in a soft tender voice. "It would hurt me...deeply."

Pride and belief in her eyes, she stared into his shocked hopeful face. Daria felt herself blushing again. She finished firmly. "You're mine. I'm yours. You wear my mark proudly, sweetheart. I want to wear yours. Now...I want you to mark me. Rub. It. In."

She saw wonder and hot hungry possession burn brightly in his eyes. Kairn swept his fingers through his thick gleaming seed. He spread his warm rich cream from Daria's shoulders to her thighs in small circles. Kairn's breath grew ragged as he massaged the silky fluid slowly into her skin. He took a long, sweet time re-learning her curves.

She rolled onto her back at Kairn's gentle urging. Daria moved her legs restlessly, her knees shifting wide apart. Kairn groaned deeply. "I adore you so, *Molindri*."

He added in a ragged whisper, "You are so pretty, my Mate. I cannot last long."

Daria arched into his reverent touch. She felt Kairn's cock jerk and throb against her, painting her inner thighs and pussy with fresh silky warmth.

His long fingers were slick with his seed. She could feel her pulse beating hard and fast in her clit. Kairn let his eyes linger on her face… on the tenderness and emotion overflowing her eyes.

Kairn then circled her sensitive bud in exquisite, wonderful torture. Over and over with rapt attention. Until her body bucked in an abandoned frenzy. Daria came apart in pleasure under the claim of his slow possessive hands.

A delicious languor washing through her, Daria settled against him. She felt his now soothing hands drift over her, smoothing his warm seed gently into her skin. She could feel the adoration radiating from his every touch. His eyes were bright with wonder.

With a sweet smile, she dropped a tender kiss on his soft fur. "Love…."

Drowsily, she whispered, "You. Rain…."

She dozed off, curled into his chest—lulled into sleep by the sure steady rhythm of his thundering hearts.

Kairn's thoughts were clear and calm. *My instincts would never let me hurt her. She comes first always.*

Kairn could not stop staring at Daria. His thoughts swirled dizzily. *My Mate. She loves me.*

Kairn laughed softly. *I do not have the words to describe a fraction of what she means to me.*

Tenderness suffused his every touch. Kairn could feel his eyes glowing ever so slightly. He stroked his hands over her back, slow and sure. His touch was carefully soft, but hungry. Her skin had a subtle blue shimmer in the faint light. His breath caught again in wonder. *She had wanted me to mark her.*

He smiled as her gentle breath stirred his short, fine fur over her teeth marks. Kairn examined his chest with growing pride. He traced her small bite marks with trembling fingers. He replayed the images imprinted in his brain with a fresh wash of pleasure.

His fingertips played over her bite. He extended his claws to deepen and widen them...and then reconsidered. He retracted them with a whimsical shake of his head. *My Daria's marks are wonderful just the way they are. I will wear her marks with pride.*

Kairn smiled as his fingers traced over her dainty bite. *Her marks are pleasurably tender and surprisingly deep. I have high hopes that they will scar nicely.*

Kairn smiled thoughtfully. *Next time...*

Adoration—and anticipation—flooded him at the tantalizing thought. *Maybe I can persuade her to make a bigger...more visible one, this time on my neck.*

His need for her, never far, started to rise. She slept soundly, peacefully on. Daria nuzzled closer with a barely audible sound. His ears flicking in bemusement, Kairn heard the tiniest endearing snore. He crooned softly in her ear, "Check."

A sweet smile danced on her lips. She was adorable. Kairn smiled tenderly, sniffing again at her tousled hair. He touched her reverently to make sure she was not another dream. *I know logically that she cannot be perfect. No one is...and yet, for me, she is. I will never put her on a pedestal—pedestals are too far removed...and distant. My Daria is too wonderfully real and warm for that. Besides...We enjoy each other's touch too much to tolerate pedestals.*

Kairn listened to his Daria breath. *She is safe...She is happy. Just as I am hers, she is mine.*

Kairn paused abruptly. *Rather, she will be mine.*

CHAPTER FIFTY

Together

S tretching luxuriously, Daria looked around with curiosity. Their bodies were entangled in the soft warm sheets. With a tender smile, she looked at the heavy weight resting easily around her waist. Daria felt him stir. The metal of his arm reflected the light as he took her hand. Kairn smiled at her with piercing sweetness. They entwined their fingers together. She squeezed his hand and felt his quick answering pressure.

Daria shifted again, wanting to look at his face. He lifted his arm as she turned onto her back. Muscles bunching smoothly in his massive chest and broad shoulders, he shifted to lean over her. His eyes were troubled.

Kairn hesitated, "I am sorry, my Daria. You trusted me. If you are patient, I will do better."

He nodded solemnly. "I will learn what you like over time."

His voice was courteous as he started to sit up. "On Lupera, what I did to you is a crime. I apolo..."

Daria stiffened as she thought quickly. She blurted out the first thing in her head. As she worked to gather her scattered thoughts, she shook her head slowly. Her voice vibrated with disbelief. "Better? You made me feel adored. I never imagined being so loved."

Daria wrapped her arms tightly around him and rested her head over his hearts. Possessively, she traced her fingers lightly over her bite marks. She found her voice and stated, quietly...firmly. "Mine."

She pressed a long hard kiss to his hearts—felt them stutter and then begin to thunder.

Daria tilted her head back and snapped fiercely. "Never apologize for what we shared! I didn't believe at first...didn't understand, but somehow we share dreams. I know what you want. You make me feel like I was all you saw...all that mattered! What we did...what I felt was so raw and honest. Together, we're magic. I finally know how I feel. I love you. And now...how could you say it's a crime?"

Kairn met her eyes squarely. His voice was deep and tender. "This was our claiming. The translators really do us an injustice. No more misunderstandings. You honor me with your honesty."

He shook his head in bemusement. "Let me be as clear. I never had any doubt. You are all that...and more. On my world, the intimacy of sharing our bodies...It is a matter of honor and respect. Such trust. Such Bonding...."

Kairn searched for a word. "Our kind does not do...Casual."

The word dripped with contempt. He let all of his long-standing guards fall. He continued softly. "What we have shared is sacred. Such Bonds only happen between claimed Mates."

His gaze softened with palpable tenderness "We Mate only once. We have not yet officially claimed each other as Mates. You deserve recognition for what you are to me."

His eyes burned a brilliant gold with memories and wonderfully raw emotion. His words seemed to linger in the air as he slowly extended his arm. The air crackled with intensity. Daria marveled with a swell of wondering tenderness. *His words. All the things he did. What he offered was love and...Kairn wanted...no...needed marriage. As simple as that. This was his proposal.*

Tears burned in her eyes, but Daria knew her smile was blinding. She placed her hand in his. She felt his fingers interlace tightly as he pulled her close. With unfettered joy, she accepted. Daria nuzzled deeper into his chest. She found her spot with a contented sigh. Her eyes drifted closed as she listened to the steady drum of his hearts.

His metal fingers teased out the tangles in her hair. His other hand made gentle forays up and down her back. He massaged in small circles along her spine. Effortlessly, he turned whatever muscles she had left into a happy melting puddle.

She rubbed her face over his chest and whispered with a tender smile. She studied him through the fan of her thick lashes. "What are we doing?"

He teased the sensitive cord of her neck with a dusting of kisses. He growled succinctly between kisses with a soft laugh. "Keeping my sanity. Bonding. My. Mate."

Daria reached up a sure hand. She murmured, wonder weaving through her tone, "My Mate."

She fingered the sensitive tips of his silky tufted ears. Daria felt his hard body surge and push urgently into her. She whispered into a wildly flicking ear, "Remember...."

She lightly ruffled the tufts of fur. "Control...."

Daria traced the tip of her finger along the sensitive curve of his ear. "Is."

She licked his quivering ear from the base to its vibrating tip. Daria blew a slow warm breath into his wildly flickering ear. "Over."

With a slow knowing smile, Daria stared into his burning eyes. She breathed in a husky whisper, "Rated."

Holding his mesmerized gaze, Daria nipped the sensitive edge of his ear sharply.

With a huge toothy grin, he tumbled her back into their bed. Kairn drank deeply of their shared laughter on her lips.

Out of their sight, a tender bud formed.

CHAPTER FIFTY-ONE

Kairn

Kairn woke, stretching luxuriously and reveling in the pleasurable slow burn in his muscles. It had been a long, truly wonderful night. They had finally drifted off to sleep only a few hours ago. A light herbal fragrance teased his nose. He turned his head trying to locate the elusive scent. Kairn saw the lush, blue vine flushed with vivid, new life. Kairn took a long deep breath with a peaceful smile.

Kairn settled back in bed. He cuddled Daria in her favorite spot against his hearts. Kairn knew he had never felt so at peace and yet... looking down at Daria's features, he could still feel the ever-simmering hunger his Mate stirred in him.

He sniffed at Daria's hair—ah...chocolate. He smiled nostalgically. *I will have to install a deep soaking tub so I can look forward to washing her hair...time after amazing time.*

His arms tightened reflexively around Daria, who murmured and cuddled closer.

His tail was wrapped loosely around her ankle. His tail tip flicked lazily. By chance, the tufted end swept across the sensitive sole of her foot. Daria's toes twitched and a sleepy giggle escaped. Intrigued, Kairn lifted his tail and sent the soft tip skittering lightly across her foot again.

Daria woke up with a startled ripple of laughter. She dove for it,trying to catch the teasing end of his tail. It danced elusively up her leg...along her sides...and over her ribs. His supple tail remained tantalizingly close, but just out of her reach.

Kairn darted his tail across her ribs, twirling the tufted end in quick light circles. Daria wriggled, trying to elude his...tickling tail.

Kairn grinned. *Tickling! That was the word for the ultimate secret weapon.*

Kairn leaned over with a wide, happy grin. "Forfeit?"

Between helpless laughter, Daria gasped out, "Name your terms."

Kairn leaned back obligingly. With a mischievous smile, Daria trailed her fingers lightly across his belly. Kairn shouted with carefree delighted laughter.

His body jackknifed off both her and the bed. He took the tangle of bedding with him, landing with a loud thump. Daria stuck her head over the side, propping her elbows on the bed. She wriggled her fingers teasingly.

Kairn's laughter faded slowly, but his smile was bright. "Draw until next round?"

Daria nodded with a playful smile. She dropped to the floor amidst the nest of rumpled blankets. She cuddled against Kairn. She wriggled until she found her spot. She leaned her head against his hearts. His arms snuggled her closer.

They were both quiet. Then, Kairn mused idly, "So...as we both know about this tickling..."

The silky tuft of his tail darted along her ribs in a teasing foray. Daria caught his tail mid length gently. Kairn's tail wound around her arm. The soft tuft brushing lightly to and fro across the soft skin at the bend of her elbow. Kairn heard Daria quickly turn her giggle into a snort.

Daria's voice was serious, but her eyes danced with laughter. "Now...just to be fair...I should get a handicap for the obvious size discrepancy."

Kairn shook his head, a smile tugging at his lips. "Neutralized since you are a battle-proven veteran...with experience and stealthy tactics on your side."

Daria sniffed. "Doesn't apply. Equalized by...hello...furry tail!"

Kairn glared, trying to hide his grin. "You routed me on the first encounter."

Daria snorted. "You're perfecting the covert attack. What's next?"

Kairn's voice was warm with humor. His eyes were tender. "What else...We negotiate."

Kairn's tail swept over her ribs.

Hunger heating his blood, Kairn leaned, closer to her. His tail slowed, became a lazy caress along the curve of her rib cage. Her breath caught. Daria tilted her head. She leaned up, her lips parting. Kairn paused. His voice was a beguiling mix of humor and hunger. "Where is Molly?"

Daria's eyes sharpened. She smiled mischievously at him. "I left our little cockblocker with Darzik."

They shared a brilliant smile. Kairn marveled to himself. *She is such a small being to hold my heart in her capable tender hands. To have found laughter, love, and shared understanding...To find such pure enjoyment in her company. Against all odds. Across countless worlds.*

Kairn cupped her jaw with a reverent hand. Turning her head into his touch, Daria nuzzled his palm with a melting smile. Kairn shook his head in renewed amazement. *I know I have been outlandishly lucky just to find her...let alone to win her heart. I will always treat her as the priceless treasure I know her to be.*

Kairn stared a moment longer, savoring the intoxicating wave of smoldering hunger and laughter surging through him. Their lips met. His tongue traced her lower lip. He smiled as he tasted her laughter.

CHAPTER FIFTY-TWO

In the meanwhile

The device at the South Pole was destroyed from a safe distance by the Luperans. The prisoners of war had likely helped save the planet by sharing what they knew. They were to receive asylum on the Guardian—under careful supervision by Darzik and Lirinx.

Upgraded sensors (specially calibrated for wormholes adapted for on planet use) were scrutinized closely to monitor for any incursions by the Ichori.

Lupera had committed to a mentorship to help Earth become a valued member of the Alliance. The Guardian was posted to Earth's orbit for the foreseeable future.

Much to his chagrin (and Darzik's eternal amusement), Kairn was now the formally recognized Luperan ambassador to the planet. He still was (predictably) incredibly nonpolitically correct—and helped build a cohesive (and collegial) United Earth government assembly.

The fragile environment was slowly righting itself with an assist from Luperan tech. Life on Earth would never be the same, but it was always worth living. The Earth and her people were healing. It was time to celebrate the good things and happy events still to be found.

EPILOGUE ONE

Daria thought of Kairn with a tender smile. He'd had Breis deliver the box. Kairn had remembered. She touched gentle fingers to the intricately carved gauntlet on her right hand. Bouncing with barely contained excitement, Molly's new collar jingled softly. Molly barked *Time to go now.*

Her translator looked like an ornate very feminine piece of frippery. Kairn had given her it as her Mating gift. He had even given her a sleek wrist comm for use at the hospital. Rumor was that he had had Breis toiling away on it for days—just to have it ready for their ceremony. Daria smiled mistily. *It really is the little things that mattered the most.*

With a gleam in his glowing eyes, Kairn had pointedly mentioned that their "brothers" had extended their bedroom...and built them a bed big enough for them to snuggle in. *I'll have to thank our Family.*

Daria smiled with wicked tenderness. She had asked a blushing Breis to scatter lavender on the sheets. She could hardly wait. *Ah... Foreplay...*

With a flare of heat and a rush of intimate memories, Daria had commissioned bottles of delicately spiced lavender honey and super-sized bottles of hair wash. Dark chocolate and lavender. She had the feeling that he'd like them. She had a Godiva dark chocolate syrup tucked away in their room for their honeymoon at their cabin. *As Kairn's wedding gift...our wedding gifts.*

Daria came back to the present when Emily elbowed her gently. Emily had only arrived that morning and was helping her wrap the

183

presents for Kairn.

Emily stiffened her spine and took a fortifying breath. Her words were very clearly enunciated. "I haven't been a very good friend. The Luperans told me what you were going through with Kairn. I don't know what to say. I just wasn't...ready. I'm sorry. I wish I could have been there for you."

Daria reached out to hug Emily gently. Always a little too slender, Emily now appeared less thin and more comfortable with herself. "It's OK. Friends understand. You don't have to physically be here to support me. I read your letter. It helped me see clearly. I'm just glad you're here with us."

Emily looked at Daria, her eyes solemn. "The way Kairn looks at you. And you at him. It makes me believe in wonderful possibilities. In love. Someday...when I'm ready, I want that for myself."

For long moments, Daria was lost in memories. She nodded dreamily to herself. "Being with Kairn is such a life changer."

Looking up, she took note of Emily's wistful smile. Thinking of the surprisingly sweet XO, Daria smiled. *When you're ready, you and Darzik will be so good together...*

At Emily's soft laugh, Daria rolled her own eyes at the understatement. "We had some challenges, but we came out stronger for it...and together...in a way I never could have imagined."

Daria mused to herself. "He's everything I never knew I wanted... and needed. I'm...*we're* very lucky."

Her smile fading, Daria was quiet. Her voice was serious. Daria said softly, "If you ever want someone to talk to..."

Emily leaned back slowly. She nodded, tears making her grey eyes shine. "I know. When I'm ready."

Emily paused and picked up a pretty crystal bottle. "So...Daria... what's with all the shampoo? It's your favorite stuff...and a fool proof gift for all your birthdays and Christmases for as long as I've known you. I thought this was Kairn's present?"

Daria shook her head ruefully. She sang out, "Deflecting much?!"

Emily grinned. "You know it. Like a champ!

Emily threw her a sly wink. "It's working, isn't it?"

They shared a look of tacit agreement. Daria thought fiercely. *Sooner than later.*

Daria finally registered Emily's words and cringed. "Don't...never call it shampoo. Please. It's hair wash."

Emily leaned closer with a mischievous grin. "So there's a reason why the labels are removed? Sounds like a good story. You're blushing..."

Molly pushed her nose insistently against Daria's palm. She yipped. *Going to be late. We need to go now...*

Emily caught Molly gently by her collar. "What's up with Molly?"

Molly snorted. *That one make us late now. I promised.*

Daria laid a reassuring hand on Molly's back. "We got an early start. Give her a minute, girl. She'll get it."

Daria smiled. "Kairn asked Molly to keep us on time. Molly takes her responsibilities seriously."

Emily shook her head as she giggled. "The way you talk to that dog..."

Emily paused; her attention caught by the collar's material. She knelt down to examine it. Emily ran her fingers over the supple length, the metal mesh marked with enamel running the spectrum of blue and interspersed with brilliant grey crystals.

The bell on the collar rang merrily. Emily chuckled. "Wow...this is a beautiful piece. No question that he knows your favorite color. What's with the bell?"

Daria replied with amusement, "The collar is Kairn's wedding present to Molly...and himself.

Emily looked up at Daria suddenly, curiosity burning in her eyes. "Why does it spell out cockblocker?"

EPILOGUE TWO

Daria felt like she floated down the walkway. Molly walked sedately at her side. She met Kairn's eyes. His lambent gaze radiated a warm, achingly tender welcome, lingering on her face. Molly's bell jingled merrily. They shared a smile. Emily took her bouquet of silver blossoms and took a small step back.

Kairn took Daria's hands in his. He squeezed them softly before he intertwined their fingers tightly. They fell into each other's gaze. Basking in the rich emotions, they were lost in their own world.

Darzik grinned, clearing his throat loudly. Kairn startled slightly. With a delighted smile, Kairn stared at his Mate for a few beats of awed silence.

His words echoed in the expectant silence. "My dreams were but a pale shadow of the shining truth that is you. Courage is not the absence of fear, but the strength and character to fight through it. My thanks for your courage and faith. You fought for us. For what humans know as love."

His gaze lighting with a steady flame, his voice rang out sure and proud. "My vow to you...I claim and protect what is mine. I defend with tooth and fang. I am steadfast and loyal. I Mate for life. *Molindri.* All that I am...With my body, I thee worship."

His voice deepened with the richness and complexity of his feelings. "I will treasure you. I am yours, my Mate. Always."

As his familiar words reverberated deep inside her, Daria stared at him in wonder. *All. This. Time.*

Kairn flashed a slow, wicked, knowing smile. Kairn showed more than a hint of sharp white teeth. His eyes glowed. With certainty, she knew she was ready.

She felt the moment he released the rigid control he exercised over his mind. Daria threw her head back and laughed in delighted wonder. She felt the questioning gentle touch of his mind...and welcomed him.

The floodgates of his mind were open. Daria felt his joy and amazement at even finding her. The depth of his trust as he showed her the forgotten details of the dreams they had shared.

She stared at him in tender bemusement. *Her quirky humor he found enchanting. He thought English slang was their thing. Her occasional awkward turn of phrase and lack of tact he found honest. Her drive to do her job well he thought honorable. He found her freckles mesmerizing and wanted to count them. Her fuller curves bewitched him. Her every touch he hoarded like treasure. He absolutely adored it when she cuddled with him.*

Daria blinked back tears of pure joy. *Kairn was ridiculously proud of her bite marks. He wanted more. Bigger and in visible places. To him, it was confirmation of her passion and joy in them. Awwwww.*

Daria remembered the ache of loneliness she couldn't explain, now dispelled forever. Her eyes brimmed with tears of happiness. *Unconditional acceptance. Pure devotion. We will always have each other. This...this is love.*

Kairn carefully caught her tears with a gentle finger. He smiled with fierce sweetness...and absolute certainty. He stated with contentment. "Happy tears."

Daria graced him with a brilliant smile that radiated happiness. She nodded her head vigorously, nearly bouncing with excitement. "Very happy tears, sweetheart."

Somehow, they had found each other. She basked in his smile and spoke aloud the vows he had now emblazoned on her heart. "We will treasure each other, my Mate. As you are mine, always I am yours."

With a tender parting squeeze, Kairn released her hands. As Kirov stepped close to Kairn, the taciturn Medico handed him a small black bag with a startlingly sweet smile.

Kairn nodded. He solemnly shook two simple rings onto his palm. They were chased with a raised relief of the vine in his quarters, which now grew in a lush latticework over the mantle.

Kairn lifted the smaller ring. He held it so she could see the bold engraving on the inside, 'Always. Mine.' and slid it carefully onto Daria's trembling finger.

Kairn then held up the larger ring, showing her the engraving, 'Always. Yours.' He placed it in Daria's palm. She carefully slid it onto his left 4th finger, feeling the faint tremor in his hand. Holding her eyes, Kairn raised the ring to his lips and kissed it tenderly. He whispered. "Always."

Kairn entwined their hands. Daria smiled through happy tears. She whispered back, tightening her grip as they shared a wondering smile, "Always. It's the little things..."

The Luperan cleric cleared his throat with an indulgent smile. He wound supple blue vines with exaggerated care around their joined hands. Soft purple leaf buds and a lone silver bud lay close along their skin.

Her mind reached out for his, the boldly intimate touch making shivers of delight...and anticipation run through them both. He whispered in her mind. *Molindri. Always. Together*

In his mind he heard her soft laughter, *Always. Best cuddle ever!*

They stared in wonder as buds rapidly grew along the vines, unfurling into a profusion of lush leaves wreathing their hands. Joy lit Kairn's eyes as a large bud slowly blossomed into a silvery flower.

EPILOGUE THREE

Emily started with surprise. Kairn had gotten them matching wedding rings to blend their commitment ceremonies. Emily watched with a tearful smile as a Luperan priest wound blue vines with a few purple leaves and a single silver bud around Kairn and Daria's tightly joined hands. Her eyes widened as leaves emerged and small buds grew. A few slowly blossomed into frothy silver flowers as the leaves richly thickened.

Bright, excited smiles dawned across the room. Kairn whispered into Daria's ears. A warm blush washed over her cheeks as they shared a look of incredulous wonder. Kairn dropped a soft kiss on Daria's head and nuzzled her hair. He brought her close in a tight embrace as she snuggled her head into his chest

Abruptly, Emily felt like she was intruding on an intimate moment between the newly Mated pair. She looked around the room for a quiet corner.

Emily watched Daria carefully. Emily nodded to herself. *Daria looked so happy. It was wonderfully obvious to everyone that Kairn and Daria were good together...and good for each other.*

She heard a steady thumping noise and registered then soft ringing of a bell. She slowly turned to a warm presence at her side. A towering black-furred Luperan stood a respectful distance away from her, Molly sitting quietly on her leash at his side.

Emily shivered. She knew she talked a good game...most of it trash. *I can do this.*

She summoned a polite smile. She had worked very hard at it. She knew she had a good mask.

She felt anxiety make her forehead shine with sweat. *Why did they all have to be so massive? He seemed to loom intimidatingly. Have none of them ever heard of personal space?*

She took two small steps away. *Surely he wouldn't notice.*

With an anxious whine, Molly's tail stopped wagging. A slow smile curved the Luperan's well-cut mouth, revealing sharp gleaming teeth. He leaned further back, calm dark eyes studying her. Without a word, he guided Molly back several steps.

Emily tried to hide her clamoring nerves, but she knew he noticed. She started slightly when he spoke. His deep voice rumbled quietly, "The Anouki vines are native to our world. They are rare. They grow when they are exposed to positive emotion. The more they grow, the richer the emotion. I have only rarely seen them bloom."

She snuck another quick look at the massively built male. She swallowed hard and reflexively took another surreptitious, careful step back. *Human men have nothing on these Luperans.*

The tall Luperan didn't move a muscle. He kept a careful distance and made no quick movements. Bemused, she thought, *This one is patient. I never would have thought he could be this gentle...or intuitive.*

Emily made herself relax slowly as his voice went on. "They honor us by letting us witness their bond. It will inspire us all."

Emily watched intently. She saw Kairn sweep Daria up closely in his arms. He spun her in a slow circle before he strode swiftly for the door, her laughter belling out behind them.

Emily saw their joy. She looked at the Luperan still quietly keeping her company. He was gently petting Molly who was leaning trustingly against his leg. He smiled and inclined his head toward Molly. "I am watching Molly for Kairn and Daria while they honeymeade."

Emily felt a soft giggle escape. "We call it a honeymoon. You are dog-sitting."

His movements carefully controlled, the Luperan slowly lifted immense shoulders in a good natured shrug. "Translator malfunction. Earth slang is posing an unexpected challenge."

He flicked an ear in mild alarm. "Kairn made no mention of sitting on Molly. I cannot see how that would be very comfortable for either of us."

Emily tried to hide her smile, but a carefree giggle startled her. She savored the nearly foreign feeling of ease she felt in the undemanding presence of the large Luperan. His lips quirked as he nodded slowly. "More slang. Thank you for being so patient. My learning curve will get steeper."

They shared a smile. Emily tilted her head. *I know he's Kairn's XO. I've seen them together at the hospital, but he looks more familiar than that. Where else have I seen him before...*

She realized with a start that his dark eyes were actually a deep, rich green. An expectant silence stretched between them—filled with a fragile hope.

His voice was soft and carefully even. "Darzik."

He stretched an arm out slowly in careful invitation. Slowly, Emily began to reach for it. She caught herself and her hand dropped stiffly back to her side. With a sharp shake of her head, Emily turned and walked quickly away.

Darzik watched closely as she swiftly vanished from his sight. She had not looked back. Not once. His claws extended and flexed slowly. Her wariness gave him pause.

Molly's nose nudged his hand. Flicking her ears in confusion, she whined softly at him. *Why wait? I can tell. She your Mate. You hunter. Follow now.*

His hand continued its gentle glide over Molly's now alert ears. His voice was soft and gentle as he advised Molly, "Small steps, my impatient friend. A good hunter knows patience will reap great rewards. Emily is not ready...not yet."

Darzik blew out a deep breath. His memories were vividly clear. Daria spoke of her with great fondness...frequently. After all the stories about her sly humor and steadfast friendship, Darzik felt he already knew her...and wanted to know so much more.

Though she had not known details, Daria had warned him about Emily's painful history. Darzik had solemnly promised her. *I would never...could never hurt Emily.*

His brother's tiny Mate had ranted on and on with Kairn indulgently smiling at her side. Daria had threatened him with a dire form of Earth torture called tickling. His faithful brother Kairn had solemnly confirmed that it was a terrible thing...right before Daria grabbed suddenly at a grinning Kairn with menacingly outstretched fingers.

Darzik could not understand how her dull, short baby claws could possibly pose a threat. Since she was now officially his sister, Darzik humored her and tried to cower convincingly—while hiding an inappropriate grin. He was pretty sure he had failed since they had both laughed with him.

Kairn had caught Daria in his outstretched arms with a tender laugh. That intimate embrace as they stared raptly into each other's eyes before breaking reluctantly apart...Daria had breathlessly whispered "rain" into Kairn's wildly flicking ears, making his eyes glow. Darzik shook his head. He still did not understand all their excitement over the common form of precipitation.

Darzik freely admitted that he frankly envied what Kairn and Daria were building. As did they all. *That Bond so rich with laughter, intense unbreakable commitment, and tenderness. To have a Mate to cherish and share my life with...it had seemed an unobtainable dream. I had never dared aspire so high...until now.*

Emily had started to visit his dreams. Flashes of her at work. Laughing with Daria. Her face set in determined lines as she fired her projectile weapon at a weapons arena.

His protective instincts rising, Darzik had made a point of watching over her. With knowing indulgent grins, Lirinx and Breis had laughingly surrendered...volunteered their slots on Emily's protection detail to him.

Darzik frowned with growing concern. Emily was so stiff and guarded. *I sense there is something dark in her past that caused her to be so wary around males. It is not subtle. Every male on her protection detail knew it. She is mine to protect, but I have to earn her trust... that will take the gift of time.*

Darzik forced himself to relax. *I know our courtship will take understanding hearts. I have to heed my own words...patience.*

He focused on a half-remembered fragment of a dream. They had been lying on bedding stretched on lush green grass. Sunlight dappling her face, Emily had been sleeping with her head pillowed on his chest.

He had been gently playing with the silky strands of her blonde hair. His hearts thumped when he remembered Emily slowly opening sleepy, trusting grey eyes and turning to him with a sweet smile.

Darzik bit his tongue hard, the taste of his blood grounding himself in this reality. He pulled his dormant cutting of Anouki vine from his belt with a careful fingers. He stared down at it, stroking a gentle claw over the new soft violet blush suffusing it with the promise of new life.

In that moment, Darzik knew hope.

EPILOGUE FOUR

D arzik touched down his transport in the far corner of the Command Base's landing area. Molly looked up with a polite wag of her tail. The big shepherd picked up her leash. She flashed a sly canine grin at him. *My Daria takes me for long walks.*

Darzik stepped off their vehicle. A knowing grin tugged at the corners of his mouth. He took a deep breath of the crisp night air. "That is why we are parked all the way out here...in the hinterlands. We are going to enjoy a good, long brisk walk back to the Base."

Darzik started toward the main buildings at a good clip. "I have been warned of your endearing habits, my friend. Lirinx regaled me with many detailed stories about you."

Molly stalked past him, her ears drooping sulkily. She picked up her pace into an easy, ground-eating trot. Darzik called after her, amusement in his voice. "Rest assured...I will be taking very good care of you while Daria and Kairn are on their Honeymeade."

Remembering Emily's shy smile, Darzik corrected himself. "Honeymoon."

Darzik unfastened his uniform jacket. He smiled to himself. *The cool tree-scented breeze does feel quite good.*

Darzik pulled a long, flat plastic disc out from where he had had it surreptitiously tucked away in his jacket. He spun it between his fingers. It made a distinctive high-pitched sound. Ears perking with eagerness, Molly's head twisted around. She barked excitedly. *I know that sound. That means lots of chasing.*

With a knowing shake of his head, Darzik threw it with a sharp twist of his wrist. *Kairn has the right of it. This innocuous little disc looks to keep Molly happily occupied for hours.*

Darzik grinned. "We may as well enjoy each other's company."

The colorful disc soared off into the night with a sharp high-pitched whirr. Molly's jaws dropped open in a wide canine grin. She dashed after it with a loud happy bark.

Darzik watched the dog's wildly wagging tail disappear into the darkness. He shook his head. *With the added benefit which I should best not mention aloud: The exercise will tire you out so you will not miss your human so much...and I may get some sleep.*

Molly trotted back with the flat disc held securely in her jaws. She laid it at his feet. Tail waving back and forth, the shepherd sank to her haunches. Tilting her head, Molly stared at him expectantly. She whined, her large paws dancing in place. *You are more fun than I expected. Throw it again.*

Darzik obligingly threw the disc. He raised a brow in admiration as Molly tore after it. *The disc is covering a decent distance. Surprisingly aerodynamic. What did Daria call it again? Fishy...Frisky...no...Frisbee. What an odd name. It does have a pleasing ring to it.*

Darzik could hear the soft thud of Molly's paws heading back toward him. As he approached the Base buildings, the breeze picked up. With a frown, Darzik sniffed the air. An unfamiliar scent tickled his nose. *There is another animal here...no...three. I do not recognize the scent profile, but they are not canine.*

Darzik broke into a sprint. *And they are very angry...and scared.*

Just ahead of him, Molly barked; the sound contained surprise and curiosity, but no fear...no anger. There was a loud angry-sounding hiss. *Stay away!*

Muttering a curse, Darzik picked up his pace even more as he ran toward the commotion. Darzik came to a sliding stop at the tableau before him.

Molly had dropped the Frisbee. Her tail was wagging gently back and forth. She sat down abruptly. The shepherd flicked a quick look at Darzik. *I am trying to look smaller. You should do the same.*

With that sage advice, Molly let her jaws drop down in a friendly, toothy grin. The shepherd lowered herself onto her belly in a careful movement. Darzik murmured as he slowly sat on the ground, "Excellent idea. Try smiling with less teeth."

Molly let her jaws close slightly. The dog yipped softly. *We mean you no harm. This one is a good two legs...though not as good as my Daria.*

Darzik stared at the small black and white animal barring Molly's way. His translator supplied blandly. The animal was a feline...and female. She was a fraction of Molly's size, but her fierce stance belied her small size and her underlying fear.

Darzik nodded with growing admiration. *Attitude is everything.*

The small feline had dull black and white fur; it was puffed around her body, making her appear far larger than her actual size. The translator identified her finally as a domestic short hair cat.

The small cat maintained her position, her wary gaze flicking from Molly to Darzik. Her long tail quivered in the air. She was panting, her dainty but very sharp fangs on display.

Darzik kept his movements easy and smooth. There was nothing more he could do about his size. He softened his voice. "Hello, little one. It is getting cool out here. It is much warmer in my quarters. The rooms are spacious...if you wanted to get out of the weather. Molly and I are hungry. We are having..."

Darzik paused, sending Molly a questioning look. The shepherd whined with resignation. *Fish would work...the fresher the better. NOT my favorite.*

The feline's long whiskers twitched; though she stood her ground, she furtively licked her lips.

There was a small scuffling sound behind her. A plaintive yowl trembled in the still air. *We have not had fish before...it sounds good.*

Two much smaller felines materialized out of the shadows. The larger one was almost pitch black. The black and white cat twisted her body, desperately trying to keep her gaze on both Darzik and the approaching smaller cats.

She spat out obvious orders. The two younger felines flattened their ears at her scolding and affixed themselves to her back paws.

Darzik gave his translator a silent order to cover all detectable languages of sentient beings on Earth. The black and white cat slowly shuffled backwards, nudging...*shepherding* her small charges back to the shadows.

Darzik activated his comm. He murmured evenly, "Kirov, I need you come to the main entrance right now. Bring some fresh meat...fish would be best. I need you to be very quiet and move slowly. We have some curious guests that I would like to entice to stay."

The largest cat turned, giving him a considering wide-eyed look. Darzik could see her ribs and spine visibly slide under her coarse fur as her coat slowly flattened. Her tongue flicked out in a tell-tale sign of longing.

Darzik could hear Kirov shuffling objects in the background. Darzik added softly, "Bring some warm milk...that bland white liquid that Daria and Kairn are so inexplicably fond of."

There was silence on the line. Kirov answered softly, "Understood. I am on my way."

Molly settled down at Darzik's side, laying her head on her front paws. Her tail thumped in a slow drum of welcome on the hard ground. Darzik flashed a quick approving grin at the big dog.

Darzik retracted his claws with a crisp snick. He met the black and white feline's wary golden gaze squarely. Darzik kept his voice carefully even. "I am called Darzik. I am stationed here. I am getting hungry. Are you?"

He smiled slightly. "My brother is bringing me some food. There will be more than enough for us to share...if you like."

Darzik was impressed by the way the black and white cat kept her body pointedly between him and the smaller animals. With a start, he realized they were mere kits. They were surprisingly plump with shiny thick fur.

Darzik stared in dawning understanding at the fiercely protective larger feline. He stated softly, "You are their guardian. You are taking care of them...at the expense of yourself."

As he shifted his body, the black and white cat hissed at him—the fur along her back standing up again. Darzik slowly stretched out his open hand. "We mean you no harm. If you let us, we would like to help you. I would like to be your friend."

Darzik let his eyes rest on the curious kits peering out from behind her thin flank. "Your kits are very pretty. They look very healthy."

Darzik paused, looking sternly into the startled black and white cat's face. "You do not."

Darzik let authority tinge his voice as he added grimly, "You cannot take good care of them if you let yourself get sick."

The thin cat hesitated. She let a huff of...Darzik hid his smile... exasperation. *That gesture does not need a translator.*

She yowled in resignation. *I am Swift Paw. You must be very good at your work...because that kind of flattery will get you nowhere.*

Swift Paw relaxed a tiny bit, her fur settling back down. She turned her head, her bright eyes openly studying him. *You are not like any two legs I have ever seen. I thought you were bringing the traveling prison. I have lost family to it before...too many. They were never seen again.*

Swift Paw hissed, her sharp fangs glinting in the low light. *Whatever it takes, I will not lose these two as well.*

Molly let out a quiet yip. *You do not know me, but Darzik is a good two legs. He has honor. He means what he says. He truly just wishes to help you... and your pups.*

Molly's jaws dropped open in an easy grin. *Your kits.*

Swift Paw yowled in amusement. *I have not spoken with a canine like this before. You are surprisingly quite tolerable.*

Swift Paw hesitated another moment. She used her tail to keep the kits gently back. Her tone softened into a meow. *They are called kittens... not kits. My only remaining brother and sister.*

Swift Paw studied Darzik's patiently proffered hand. The kittens squeaked, bouncing up and down with barely contained excitement. She threw a stern warning glance back at the kittens as they tried to stealthily creep forward. Swift Paw took a small step. Darzik kept himself very still, keeping his hand outstretched and as unthreatening as he could make a hand as massive as his appear.

Swift Paw's flattened ears slowly perked up. With a soft yowl, she covered the remaining distance with small, guarded steps.

The thin cat hesitantly laid a light paw on Darzik's palm. Taking care not to make any sudden moves and telegraphing his intentions, Darzik slowly reaching over with his other hand. He lightly rubbed under her jaw and felt a steady vibration thrum to life under his careful fingers; a low pleasant sound filled the quiet.

Swift Paw rubbed her head into Darzik's hand with a soft sound of relief. *Trust does not come easily to me, but there is something different about you. You are very different from any other two legs.*

Swift Paw stared intently into Darzik's eyes. She purred even more loudly. *I am learning that different is very good.*

Swift Paw lowered her guard completely, leaning into Darzik's careful hand. She yowled imperiously. The kittens lurched forward with excited mewls, climbing and tumbling over each other repeatedly in their hurry.

Darzik grinned up at Kirov. Leaning against a wall, the taciturn Medico had been watching their introductions from a short distance away for the past several Earth minutes. He was equipped with a large hamper. His usually stern features were softened by a wondering smile.

Eyes widening, the black kitten sniffed the air suddenly. Her head whipping toward Kirov in astonishment, the kitten skidded to an unexpected halt. Unable to stop in time, her littermate careened into her. The small black kitten wobbled, before over balancing and landing awkwardly on a small, jagged rock.

The kitten let out a quickly cut-off squeak of pain. Darzik started to get up, but Kirov quickly scooped up the young cat. The Medico's voice was uncharacteristically gentle. "Who have we got here?"

Swift Paw checked her head-long rush over as Kirov cradled her sister in a large careful hand. She flicked Darzik an amused look. She settled back next to him, leaning unconsciously into his scratching fingers. The thin cat and the imposing Luperan made an odd sight as they watched the adorable interactions unfolding before them.

Kirov frowned slightly as he evaluated the tiny animal in his hand. The Medico's long fingers probed gently, running through the kitten's soft, thick fur with a light touch. The kitten turned bright blue adoring eyes up to Kirov. *That feels nice. Do not stop.*

The kitten hissed sharply as Kirov's fingers paused. Her tiny sharp claws dug into his skin reflexively—drawing tiny beads of blue blood. The kitten's ears drooped. She retracted her claws with a chastened dip of her small head. Her yowl was saturated with regret. *I am sorry. I did not mean to do that. I am still learning my manners. Sometimes I forget.*

Shaking his head with a grin, Kirov rumbled quietly, "Do not worry about the tiny scratch. I have thick skin...and I have had far worse. Let us get you tended to."

Retrieving a portable cryogen wand from his jacket pocket, Kirov swept it over the small kitten curled trustingly in the palm of his hand. The kitten stretched. Her eyes widened. *That made the hurt go away. I do not know how you did that, but...thank you.*

She started purring. The sound was amazingly loud for her small size. *I like you. I am Far Eye.*

Kirov hesitated, his dark blue eyes lightening with startled pleasure. "I like you too. Far Eye is a good name."

The small cat lifted her head with an endearing air of disgruntlement. Her bright eyes unblinking, the kitten stared at him expectantly. *You are not very good at this. It is your turn.*

She wrapped her short whippy tail around his thick wrist as far she could. *You are supposed to tell me your name now. How will I know what to call you otherwise?*

Openly charmed, Kirov's eyes warmed even more. His grin was wide and carefree. "How remiss of me. I have forgotten my manners. I am not allowed in public often for good reason. I am called Kirov. I am glad we are friends."

Far Eye gazed at him reproachfully. She meticulously picked her way up to a lofty perch on his shoulder. She batted at his cheek lightly, claws carefully sheathed. She purred madly, rubbing against Kirov's jaw. *That too. Friends are good, but we are more than that.*

The kitten's blue eyes filled with affection and wonder. *You are my brother...my very big brother. We are Family.*

Even without a translator, Darzik could have read Swift Paw's bemusement. Swift Paw huffed indulgently. *Out of the mouth of a kitten. I am used to such wisdom...but usually out of the other one. Family...you do not have to born into it.*

Darzik met Swift Eye's calm gaze. "Kirov...the rest of my bridge crew... they are my chosen brothers. Stay a while. As you said, blood does not define Family. There is always room for more. Family is everything..."

Swift Paw looked at Far Eye climbing happily all over Kirov...at the other kitten...her brother peacefully dozing off between Molly's paws. She nodded slowly.

Swift Paw felt a storm of affection...hope...and safety as she looked at her unlikely two-legged brother towering over her. The young cat purred softly, wonder tinging her tone. *Family...*

Darzik looked at Kirov as their deep laughter mixed with the contrasting purrs and barks. Darzik reached into his belt. With reverent fingers, he slowly drew out his Anouki vine fragment.

The light violet of the vine was now easily visible. The stem was now noticeably supple and beginning to dapple with subtle shades of ethereal purple. He traced the tip of his finger along the short length. *Surely not...*

Darzik paused, tracing the stalk again. He felt it warm again...ever so slightly. His skin tingled pleasantly.

Looking down, his eyes widened. The fragment was indeed slightly longer. Darzik blinked. He imagined he could feel the merest suggestion of tiny leaf buds along its still thin length. Darzik looked over at Kirov sharply.

Darzik showed the Medico what he held so carefully in his hand. Kirov studied the young living vine in awe. He reached out a tentative finger before letting it fall back to his side with a soft sigh.

Kirov stared at him with slowly lightening eyes. Kirov drew in a long breath. He flashed a solemn look at Darzik. "We have spoken of your Emily. I fear she has deep wounds that we cannot see."

Kirov gave him a sharp look. "Your courtship will take time."

Darzik nodded slowly. "I know. My Mate is well worth any wait."

Kirov smiled softly. "You will be good for her. You...like Kairn... deserve every happiness. My hearts are glad for you, brother."

Darzik looked down at his hand. The fragment glowed a rich blue against his grey skin. A small bud ripened in front of his wondering eyes...unfurling into a tiny purple leaf.

Molly's stomach rumbled loudly, shaking them out of their reverie. Her tongue lolled out as she sniffed the air. *Something smells good..*

Tucking the precious vine back in his belt, Darzik lifted his jaw toward the forgotten hamper. With an eager bark, Molly dashed off. She set it gently down between Darzik and Kirov. The Medico dropped to the ground gracefully. Darzik smiled, noting the careful hand Kirov kept around his exploring kitten. The Luperans emptied the capacious hamper.

They set out platters of salmon...a whole roasted chicken...slices of cheese...bowls brimming with cream. The kittens stared at the growing mountain of food in wide-eyed stunned silence.

With a conspiratorial grin, Darzik gave Molly a large shank bone. With a bark of gleeful thanks, the shepherd began to gnaw on it contentedly.

Kirov lay a sizable chunk of salmon and a bowl of cream in front of the kittens. Far Eye let out a delighted mewl, slicing off a small sliver of the fish.

She took a small enthusiastic bite. Far Eye stopped chewing. She looked up at them, a look of utter bliss on her face. She started purring madly. *I like fish.*

The male kitten lapped neatly from the bowl of cream. Looking up, he carefully licked the mustache of cream off his mouth. He wove tight figure eights around Darzik's feet. His golden eyes blinked shyly at him. *I am Peacekeeper. This is so good. Thank you.*

Darzik smiled at Peacekeeper. His eyes narrowed in thought. "I know someone who will adore you."

Peacekeeper purred in contented agreement. *You do. She is very special. Mates just are. You are waiting for her—while she waits for you. Two legs make the simplest things so complicated...*

Peacekeeper gave him a look wise beyond his tender age. *I look forward to finally meeting her.*

Taken aback, Darzik stared at the small kitten. Peacekeeper looked back with an enigmatic feline smile. In the blink of an eye, Peacekeeper reverted to kittenhood. He took a small bite of the salmon that Far Eye insistently nudged over to him with an encouraging meow. A companionable silence fell as the kittens fell to their dinner with enthusiasm.

Exchanging broad grins with Kirov, Darzik relaxed—watching the kittens enjoy their first taste of fish.

Keeping a watchful eye on the kittens, Darzik sat down next to Swift Paw. Keeping his movements slow, he ran his hand gently down her back. With a worried frown, he realized he could count her ribs easily.

Darzik stated quietly. "There is more than enough for all of us...

even as much as Kirov and I can consume. You need to eat."

Darzik heard a loud grumble from Swift Paw's stomach. Her ears flattened as she looked away in abject embarrassment. Darzik added, "You are too thin. This is *not* a criticism. You have done a wonderful job caring for them. It is..."

He searched for words. "More than acceptable for you to take care of yourself..."

They watched the kittens curl up next to each other in a furry pile. Darzik paused as Swift Paw pushed her head into his chest with a huff of relief. She meowed softly. *Soon.*

Reaching out, Darzik snagged a thick chunk of salmon. He dangled the delicacy in front of Swift Paw. Darzik countered firmly, "Now."

Her whiskers twitching, the small cat stared at it with painful longing. For long seconds, her gaze darted between him and the tempting morsel of fish.

Darzik growled softly. "You cannot keep this pace up. I will not hurt you...or your littermates. You have to trust someone. Choose me."

Darzik could see the conflict in Swift Paw's exhausted gaze. The cat wavered. Keeping her eyes on him, she slowly accepted it from his hand. With a quiet smile, Kirov promptly passed over a bowl still brimming with cream. Another juicy chunk of salmon materialized in Darzik's hands...and so it continued. Between the two of them, they fed Swift Paw until she could barely stay awake.

Swift Paw stared up at him with drowsy slitted eyes. She purred. *Did not expect this...or you. Trust you. Choose you. We are Family...brother.*

With that bombshell, she turned in a slow circle on his chest. With a soft purr, Swift Paw curled into the convenient curve of Darzik's elbow. With a slow wondering smile, Darzik retracted his claws, petting her rough fur with gentle fingers. The cat stared at him, her purr growing louder. Swift Paws stretched slowly before she kneaded his uniform coat into a small ball and trustingly went to sleep.

Kirov raised a brow. He glanced at the kittens snoozing obliviously in a boneless pile. Unconsciously, a sweet smile curved his mouth. He gave Darzik a sideways glance. "What just happened here, brother?"

Darzik grinned, lightly petting a peacefully napping Swift Paw. "I think, Kirov, we have been lucky enough to be adopted."

And thus, over a midnight snack of fresh salmon and cream, the resilient seed of a new Family was formed...

OUR FAMILY THUS FAR

Kairn:
- Mate to Daria
- Luperan
- Commander of Guardian
- Silver hair
- Amber eyes

Daria:
- Mate to Kairn
- Human
- Lead Critical Care doc in ICU

Molly:

- Female German Shepherd mix
- Familiar to Daria

Kirov:
- Luperan
- Gruff Medico on Guardian
- Incredible healer
- Awful bedside manner
- Bronze-gold hair
- Blue eyes

Darzik:
- Luperan
- Executive officer on the Guardian
- Familiar to Swift Paw
- Black hair
- Green eyes

Breis:
- Luperan
- Chief Engineer on Guardian
- Auburn hair
- Purple-blue eyes

Lirinx:
- Luperan
- Chief of Security
- Mahogany hair
- Red-brown eyes

Emily:
- Human
- Daria's best friend
- Kick-ass ICU nurse

ACKNOWLEDGMENTS

To Jessica and Thomas, the children of my heart. To my agent and dear friend, Kathryn Raaker, thank you for all the support. To Mary Lou Fornehed, Dana Kilgore, Tara Walker, Shauna Mack, Kathy Horn, and Chandel McCann for being unofficial B-readers and the best friends I could ask for. To the ICU nursing staff and office nurses, you are my heroes!

ABOUT THE AUTHOR

Fionne Foxxe Farraday is a medical professional working in the area of pulmonary and critical care medicine. After years of working with patients, Farraday faced medical issues in March 2020 that put her on forced medical leave without call responsibilities. An avid reader, she soon exhausted her list of books and found herself bored with TV, leading her to begin outlining the story that would become *Kairn: Mates of the Alliance*. Returning to ICU work during the dark days of the first Covid-19 wave, Fionne continued writing as a way to cope with the intense demands and the losses of countless patients. The writing took on a life of its own as Farraday fashioned the fictional happy endings which were in short supply in an ICU full of Covid-19 patients.

With her own background in medicine and family members who served in WWII and Vietnam, Farraday's books are a salute to all of the medical and military personnel whose sacrifices allow us to do what we do. A mother, grandmother, and animal lover, Fionne Foxxe Farraday lives outside of Nashville, TN.

WWW.MATESOFTHEALLIANCE.COM

FUTURE BOOKS

Book 2: Darzik

Book 3: Lluvallyn

Book 4: Kirov

Book 5: Gaherith

Book 6: Stacie

Book 7: Breis

Book 8: Bright Eyes

www.ingramcontent.com/pod-product-compliance
Lightning Source LLC
Chambersburg PA
CBHW060921250626
47159CB00008B/3104